For as long as I can remember, my family has been on a budget. When you're a little kid, stuff like that doesn't matter. But last year, when everyone else had this very specific kind of jeans, I had to get mine at Valu-Plus. I would rather die than tell anyone I bought jeans at Valu-Plus. I never even told Chelsie.

"I'm trying to cut back on luxuries," Dad said, pulling out the *second* box of macaroni and cheese. "Banana Flakes are luxuries. But you haven't lived till you've tried my Econo-Beans-and-Franks."

I didn't think this was funny.

"Is that on tonight's menu?" I asked. "If it is, I think Chelsie might want me to eat over at her house."

Dad didn't think that was funny, either . . .

JUST VICTORIA

Shelly Nielsen

Chariot Books
DAVID C. COOK PUBLISHING CO.

A White Horse Book
Published by Chariot Books,
an imprint of David C. Cook Publishing Co.
David C. Cook Publishing Co., Elgin, Illinois
David C. Cook Publishing Co., Weston, Ontario

JUST VICTORIA
© 1986 by Shelly Nielsen

Cover illustration by Gail Roth
Design by Barbara Sheperd Tillman

Printed in the United States of America
90 89   5 4

Library of Congress Cataloging-in-Publication Data

Nielsen, Shelly, 1958—
  Just Victoria.

  (A White horse book)
  Summary: The summer after sixth grade, Vic tries to
prepare for seventh grade so she won't be a nerd, has
problems with her best friend, and worries about her
grandmother's health.
  I. Title.
PZ7.N5682Ju 1986   [Fic]   86-2294
ISBN 0-89191-609-1

for Scott—
with love and at least
a million thanks

1

Most kids would be thrilled if it were their last day of sixth grade.

I wasn't even close to being thrilled, another perfect example of how I'm not always just-like-other-people. It's weird. If everyone else seems to be happy doing A, Victoria Hope Mahoney will be off trying out B.

But that particular day, things had moved along pretty normally. In Ms. Runebach's class we had spent the morning handing in books and stuff. It didn't even seem like school. A bunch of us argued about who got to keep Hans the science rat over the summer. I dropped out after a while, knowing my parents would not be excited about a two-pound rodent in the house. My brother is bad enough.

I ate lunch with Chels. Chelsie Bixler is also not-like-other-people, which is one reason she's my best friend.

"Don't look now," Chels told me, biting down on a slab of limp pizza, "but Peggy's on her way over here. Act casual."

Even two tables away, you could smell Peggy Hiltshire's cologne. And she looked great, if you want to know the truth. She came over in her little knockout outfit and crowded in at our table.

"Hi, you two," she said in her best Mississippi drawl. Peggy moved here years ago, but she sounds more like a character from the "Dukes of Hazzard" every day. Sometimes I want to shake her and say, "You're in Minnesota now!" I don't know why it bugs me so much.

"Pull up a seat and dig into your lunchroom rat poison," said Chels. "It's especially nauseating today."

"Last chance to O.D. on soggy green beans," I added.

"Stop that; you're making me sick," Peggy said, giggling. My heart, which had tightened itself up into the size of a frozen baby pea when I saw Peggy coming, suddenly softened.

Peggy opened a paper napkin and put it over her food. "This is a mercy mission," she said, stuffing a straw into her milk carton. "I came over to prepare you for next year."

8

"Next year!" Chelsie snorted. "Who cares about next year? Summer starts today, at exactly 3:10, and I'm not even going to *think* about school for three whole months."

"Right," I added.

Peggy took a petite bite of pizza and chewed as though she had all the time on this green earth. "I'd think about it, if I were you. My sister's going into eighth grade next year, and she told me all the gruesome details. Cutting up frogs in biology, things like that. And that's just the beginning. She says that everyone in junior high is into drugs. People who aren't get treated like kids, and they don't get into the best cliques—you know, groups. Of course," she added, with a glance at me, "you can't dress like you're in elementary school if you want to be in a good clique."

I looked at Chels, hoping for a comeback.

"Doesn't bother me," Chels said, cool as iced tea. "Does it bother you, Old Vic?"

"Not a bit." This was a lie, because my heart was pounding and I had started to sweat.

"Oh, *I'm* not worried," Peggy said quickly. "But I figure we could all use all the prep time we can get. I'm not going to be in a mediocre clique just because I wasn't ready for seventh grade." Suddenly she leaned toward Chels and asked in her most serious southern voice, "Do you think your braces will be off by September? You don't want to have braces in junior high, do you?"

9

You could have strangled on the silence.

"Peggy, don't be a clod!" I practically shouted. "Chelsie is very sensitive about her braces. They'll be off in thirteen and a half months, and in the meantime please keep quiet about them!"

Peggy said some people were sure huffy, and she had to go put on more cologne or something. She left.

Chels and I walked around the playground awhile, but she didn't feel like talking. I said one thing to try cheering her up: "Maybe you'll get your braces off early for good behavior!" But Chels and I both knew that when your father is an orthodontist, you don't get your braces off a minute before he says you'll get them off.

Lunch was over, and we headed back to our last afternoon in Ms. Runebach's sixth-grade class.

2

"We're cooked, Vic," Chelsie said. "There's only one way out of this fix—become dropouts."

I was stuffed with last-day party treats, and our usual shortcut through the ravine—which is really more of a gutter between two little slopes—was jiggling cupcakes and chocolate milk around in my stomach.

"You can't drop out of school in the sixth grade. Besides, you know how Peggy exaggerates. Maybe she made up all that stuff about cliques and frogs."

"Maybe. But what about the braces? Vic, Do you think I'm too much of a dog to go into seventh grade? I mean, with these braces? Be honest."

A feeling like the flu moved to my head. Chelsie

Bixler had nothing to worry about. Chels was *made* for junior high.

Never mind the braces—she's really good looking, the kind of person who would look glamorous in a hurricane, like a model. She can put on a plain old skirt and say something like, "This is all wrong for my skin color" or, "Straight skirts make me look like I have no waist."

I would never say anything like that. Number one, because I have a pretty funny body. If you want to know the truth, it's been a real disappointment in the growing-up department.

"Give me a break," I said. "You're great. *I'm* the one who should worry."

"Don't start that again."

"It's true." My voice snagged on the beginning of a sob. I breathed hard. My legs kept walking, but they went all wavy through the tears.

"The trouble with you, Victoria Hope Mahoney, rising star of the literary world, is that you have a poor self-image."

"A what?"

"You don't like yourself. Like that character in *The Glass Menagerie,* what's her name—?"

"All I know is, cutting my hair was the biggest mistake I ever made in my life."

"Vanity, vanity," Chelsie said in a very dramatic voice. "I've got these crummy braces, and you don't hear me griping about them day and night."

"I most certainly do!"

12

For the first time since lunch, Chels gave me an honest-to-goodness Chelsie Bixler wide-as-the-ocean grin. It's a smile you remember if you've seen it once.

We cut a sharp right. This is where I live, in the house that even Dad calls "the homeliest place in Hazelberg County." You've never seen an uglier house. With all the great places we could have lived, how did my family end up in this house on this street? Our house is the color of whipped spinach, no lie. Somebody picked it out a long time ago, so it is not only a sickening color, it's a faded-out, peeling, disgusting, sickening color. But the bent chain link fence takes your mind off it. And the driveway has the biggest cracks in the whole neighborhood, cracks like gullies.

I lifted the squeaky fence latch and walked fast to the front door. Inside, everything was normal.

"Matthew!" I yelled. "You left the door unlocked again!"

"Sorry," he yelled back, but he didn't sound sorry. He turned the TV louder.

We dumped our stuff and followed the blare into the family room. My brother, Matthew Mahoney, was watching TV in his favorite position, his body draped upside down on the couch and his feet sticking straight up in the air. He's five.

"Listen, Matthew, someone could just walk in. I keep telling you to be more careful."

"I forgot. Don't bug me." Then he noticed that

13

he had an audience. "Hi, Chels! Want to see a double backwards roll?"

Chelsie is very decent about things like her friends' little brothers, so she said, "Sure thing."

He knocked himself out tumbling, and Chels acted like it was the best show she'd ever seen. Like it was the Shrine Circus or something. She wouldn't even agree with me when I muttered, "Brothers are a pain."

"Matthew's not," she said. "Matthew's a stitch."

Chelsie doesn't have any brothers or sisters.

We climbed over the paint-splattered drop cloths and the paintbrushes and thinner and the buckets and steel wool and jars of wood putty to the kitchen, my parents' latest fix-up project.

"Wow, Vic. Your parents are really into this. Where do they get their energy? I mean, with full-time jobs and everything."

"For a start, they make *me* fix dinner."

"Tossing a salad is not 'making dinner,' my dear."

"Okay, okay, not the whole dinner. But the salads, anyway."

Due to a rule in our house that everyone pitches in, I have become an expert tossed salad maker. I have a system of four easy steps: SWAP.

1. Slice cucumbers.   3. Add tomatoes.
2. Wash lettuce.   4. Peel carrots.

"Well, maybe you should be glad your parents trust you," Chels said with a sigh. "Mom is so particular about everything. She says I might leave out an important ingredient or something, but I bet I'd be a good cook."

Chels grabbed the peeler and went after a carrot. When she started eating the lopsided tomato slices as fast as I could cut them, we got laughing so hard we were gasping when Mom arrived.

"What's with *you* two?"

We couldn't talk, so she just leaned against the refrigerator door, smelling like her wild flower cologne and looking happy.

Chels got ahold of herself first. "Sorry, Mrs. Mahoney. Old Vic breaks me up."

"Eating with us, Chelsie?"

"If that's okay."

"Sure it's okay. It's more than okay." Mom leaned over my shoulder and groaned. "Tossed *again?* You need to branch out. How about a sunflower-plum salad or a bean sprout salad with yogurt dressing? Boy, just talking about all that good food makes me weak. I've been hungry all day. Had this craving for grapes, could have died for grapes. They're very good for you. Did you know that?" She kicked off one tennis shoe, then the other, and dug around in the refrigerator awhile. "Doesn't look like we have any. Guess I'll settle for this old zucchini bread." She bit into the bread and chewed.

Chels gave me a look. My mom is extremely talkative. Dad said that she made one PTA meeting run an hour overtime when she stood up to share her vision for improved shelving in the library. Dad, however, has been known to exaggerate.

Chels picked up her peeler again, and we were all making salad like crazy when Dad came in, humming and carrying a bulging bag of groceries.

"Well! Look at this! Master chefs at work."

He looked very clean cut in his pressed white shirt. Dad says that in the old days he was a real hippie. Long hair and everything. But when he started studying to be a chef, he either had to cut his hair or wear a hairnet. *That* was when he and the barber got to be friends.

"Tossed salad again, Victoria? Ugh. I can see that someone needs a few cooking lessons to get her out of a very sorry rut. How come my expert chefdom hasn't rubbed off on my offspring?"

"It's *healthy* anyway," Mom said in my defense.

"It's boring. Hey, Chel-se-ah, glad you could join us."

"Chelsie," she corrected, but with a grin.

"Oh, right, I forgot." He twirled a pretend moustache. "I'm glad you're here, because tonight I create for vous such a feast! I create for vous, ze crepe!"

"Aren't ze crepes hard to make?" I asked, tossing the salad by flipping it out of the bowl and catching it—until Chels started giggling hysterically and Mom said "Stop that."

"On the night of my daughter's graduation from sixth grade," Dad announced grandly, "no culinary effort is too extreme. Let the festivities begin!"

It was a wonderful party. Matthew told only one knock-knock joke, and it wasn't half-bad. Mom told the story of her first date with Dad. ("He invited me to a home-cooked dinner, and the first thing he brought out were *live* clams. They *shriveled* when he squeezed lemon juice on them. I never wanted to see him again.") There was angel food cake with strawberries and whipped cream for dessert, and as a final treat, Mom said Chelsie could sleep over, if she wanted.

Chelsie looked at me. "They'll say no."

"Let's go ask," I said. "I'll walk you home."

"It won't do any good."

Please, Chels, don't spoil it. Not tonight. My stomach ached from laughing at Dad's silly jokes, and even Peggy's gloomy predictions seemed like a memory far away.

"Come on." I rushed her outside and out to the sidewalk. "Don't be a gloom ball."

Outside it was trying hard to be summer, but the breeze made me button up another jacket snap.

As we got closer to The Circle, where Chelsie's family lives, I put my hands in my pockets and stuffed my chin into my collar. The Circle is a nice subdivision six blocks from our neighborhood. Chelsie's parents do not have a thing about fixing up old houses.

Here the houses had brass numbers and perfect green lawns, every one greener than the last. The

17

fences were white picket, not bent old chain link, and you've never seen so many fresh coats of paint. Any color you could imagine; even lavender, Chelsie's favorite. There wasn't a curling piece of paint for blocks.

We passed a guy scrubbing a red sports car in his driveway. "Plays basketball for the senior high," Chels hissed at me. She straightened up, flinging her hair over a shoulder. Sometimes I think Chels is going boy crazy on me. Peggy's warning started to creep back with the cold.

Chelsie's house was hiding, cool and creamy white, under a cluster of thick crouching trees, and she motioned me in.

"Come *on*," Chels said, seeming like her old self again.

I followed her through the hallway with the mirrors, the vase of purple silk flowers, and the French doors leading to the garden. The smell of cedar and lilacs deepened like perfume.

Mrs. Bixler looked up from some bookwork she was doing at the kitchen table. I tried not to stare at all the hanging plants, the tiny color TV on the counter, the shiny copper pots and pans dangling from the ceiling.

"Hi, Mrs. Bixler," I said politely.

"Hello, Victoria. How are you?" Very polite.

"Mom, may I stay over at Vic's tonight?"

"I thought we settled this earlier," Mrs. Bixler said evenly, with a pleasant smile. For a shorter woman, Mrs. Bixler has a voice that makes you feel she's about six feet tall. It makes you stand up and take notice.

"Please, Mom? It's kind of a last-day-of-school celebration."

To make a long, kind of embarrassing story short, Chels walked me to the front door after her mom decided she better not come back to our house. The sky had darkened another shade. I stood there with her, but I didn't exactly look at her face.

"I don't think your mom likes me," I said.

"Don't be a gloom ball," Chels said. "Meet me at the new school. Tomorrow. Nine o'clock."

"Okay," I said.

"Bye."

"Bye."

3

"*You're* moody today."

Dad slid two fried eggs onto my plate and peered into my face. The eggs stared up at me, too, like a pair of yellow eyes. Sighing, I freckled them with pepper and salt.

"Not moody, Dad. Thinking."

"Thinking? What about?" The collar of his ratty old robe was folded under, and his hair stuck up. He looked like a clown. I smirked without meaning to, and he smiled too and sat down to butter his pumpernickel toast.

I knew he expected it, so I bowed my head and sat silently. But I wasn't really praying.

"I just want to know one thing." Viciously, I

chopped an egg to bits. "Is there any chance we'll be moving to The Circle in the near future? I wouldn't mind if we moved."

"When you can live in a place of vast character and history?" Dad spread his arms, Moses style.

"I just think it's highly possible that I would be a lot more popular in junior high if I lived in The Circle."

"Name one person who would like you better if you lived in The Circle."

"Peggy Hiltshire."

"Who, pray, is Peggy Hiltshire?"

"Just a girl."

"A stuffy girl, I'll wager."

Mom shuffled in, then, so he didn't get a chance to start on old Peggy.

"Welcome to the new day, Sunshine," Dad called to her.

Mom is not what you'd call a morning person. She gave him a look, and went to rummage noisily in the pantry for her herbal tea.

"Our daughter would like to move out of this latest lovely residence."

"I can't imagine why," said Mom.

"She wants to move to The Circle."

"It's not just The Circle," I said. "It's *stuff*." I thought very carefully about what I would say next, because Dad can be touchy about the subject of money. "Stuff like the Bixlers have. They're kind of rich, and we're—"

"Now I get it!" Dad pointed a toast triangle at me and got pink in the face. "If we were wealthy, Peggy Hiltshire and the Bixlers and everybody else would think we were great people. That really burns me up."

Mom touched him on the shoulder. "Don't get riled up, honey."

"I'm not riled up. I'm outraged! To think a daughter of mine—"

"Dad," I said, "this is important! Peggy gave me the scoop about junior high school yesterday. In addition to some pretty depressing stuff about frogs and cliques, she also looked right at me and said, 'Of course, you can't dress like you're in elementary school.'"

Mom was smiling. "Up until yesterday you *were* in elementary school. I don't see why you shouldn't dress like it."

"Peggy doesn't. Peggy dresses like an eighth grader at least."

"There are lots more important things in life than *stuff*. What's in a person's heart, for instance."

"Only an ignoramus would judge you by your house or your clothes," Dad grumbled.

Speaking of the clothes some people will wear—Matthew came in just then, wearing his fuzzy alligator slippers. His hand was stuffed into a cereal box. He came up behind my chair, smelling like wet cereal.

"It's a good day for going to the zoo," he said.

"I'm not going to the zoo with you, Matthew, so stop hinting."

"Watch me!" he said. "I can do a double backwards roll."

Mom and Dad clapped and oohed and aahed. I just fumed.

"Don't be a spoilsport, Victoria," Dad said. "There's another reason that a sudden move across town isn't likely. It's an excellent reason. Which brings us to an important news flash." He squeezed Mom's hand.

I blinked, and my stomach dropped like it was on an elevator. *A baby. We're having another baby.*

"It's about my job," Mom said.

I tried very hard not to sound too relieved. "A raise, Mom?"

"A whole new job. I applied for an opening in Willowood's new counseling department, and they decided to hire me."

Matthew shoveled more dry cereal into his mouth. "That's neat."

I may not be the brain of the universe, but the light was starting to dawn. This had something to do with moving to The Circle. "Is this a step up or a step down?"

"Depends on how you look at it. Maybe a step down from the travel agency, financially. But it's what I'm trained for. Also what I've always wanted to do." Her eyes turned into little half moons behind her grinning cheeks. "Seems like a pretty good use of time for an ex-hippie."

I should have seen it coming. My parents had been talking a lot about the poor old people at Willowood, the nursing home a couple blocks away. "Think how lonely they must be," Mom's always saying. "Losing their homes, their families, their friends."

I hate nursing homes.

I have hated nursing homes since the Bixlers almost put Chelsie's grandma in one after her stroke.

"Does this mean The Circle is out?" I asked, completely losing my appetite for eggs.

I had gone too far. Mom gave me a look that was angry, plus a little hurt.

"The Circle was never *in*. If you have any good reasons why I shouldn't take the job, tell me now, so we can talk about it."

Dad joined in. "We want you to be happy. But I for one don't think The Circle is our ticket to fulfillment."

"I was just kidding," I said.

"Here. Truce. I'll pour you a tantalizing cup of Terry Mahoney's spiced coffee brew, and we can be friends again."

Mmm. Cinnamon. I breathed deep over the black and breakfasty coffee Dad poured in my mug, and took a tiny sip. In this family there are always surprises to keep you interested and maybe just a little worried about what will happen next.

Things like cinnamon coffee and Mom suddenly working at a nursing home.

"You're not going to let your daughter put that caffeine in her system!" Mom protested. But I was too quick to let that old argument get going.

"I think it's really great, Mom," I interrupted. "About your job, I mean."

As long as no one made *me* go to Willowood Nursing Home. Nursing homes give me the creeps.

4

As usual, Chelsie was late. I sat on the curb examining the little hairs on my legs and every once in a while looking up at the silent black letters on the glass marquee: KEATS JUNIOR HIGH SCHOOL. Someone had thrown rocks through. The message underneath was a laugh. "HaVe a nic summeR!" Except I didn't feel like laughing.

I cut through the parking lot, pretending that I belonged here, and trying to imagine myself with books in my arms, my hair grown out. Slick. Mature.

A couple guys in the baseball diamond out back were tossing a ball back and forth, catching it in their mitts. First one. *Smack!* Then the other.

Smack! I kept waiting for a miss: a *Smack!* followed by silence, the ball rushing at me like a meteor. I walked faster, my skin crawling. The ball never skipped a beat, but as I turned the corner, I thought I heard laughter—deep, boys' laughter. I didn't turn around.

"Where have you been?" It was Chelsie.

She looked different. Her hair was piled up on her head, and the effect was pretty spectacular, even if one side was toppling out. Her lips were this wild pumpkin color that didn't match her lavender shorts.

"Just experimenting," she explained. "Mom doesn't know about the lipstick."

"I—I like your earrings," I said.

"Oh. Thanks." She pushed each lobe toward me till the pink gems flashed. "Mom and Dad gave 'em to me last night. Graduation present. Did your parents get you anything?"

I considered lying my face off. "Well. The dinner, I guess."

"That was the best dinner I ever had in my life. It beat Chicken Kiev hands down. And I happen to think Chicken Kiev is delicious."

We checked the place out, weaving through a few parked cars in the lot. The morning was getting to that heavy, hot hour just before noon. Already the sun was blistering, giving us tans. So this is what we'd been missing all spring in Ms. Runebach's class while we were listening to the

27

sounds of chalk scratching on the board and flies buzzing at the windows. I was glad it was finally summer, Keats or no Keats.

"What's that?" said Chels suddenly, lifting her head, as we headed around the side of the building. "Do you hear it?"

"That" was old Peggy Hiltshire, bouncing around out in the football field. She had a couple of her friends with her, and they were all jumping up and down and shouting strange things. She saw us watching and came dashing over.

"Well, *hi*, you all. Oooooh, I *love* your earrings." She grabbed Chelsie's ear to see one up close. "They're real, aren't they?"

"Yeah, I guess."

"Well, they're grand. I might get a pair just like them."

I felt glued to the asphalt. Heat waves on the soft tar reflected back up my bare legs.

"What're you doing here?" Peggy said with a grin, slicing a look over at me. "Checking out junior high? Checking out all the stuff I told you about?"

"Just looking the place over," said Chels. "A little investigative journalism."

"There's one more thing. My sister just told me. We have to take showers after gym class. You know, get naked in front of everyone."

Chels and I gave each other looks.

"That's disgusting." Chelsie leaned over the sidewalk and made retching noises.

Peggy raked her fingers through her hair, and every ravishing wave fell back in place. "They want gym class showers, they'll get 'em. I'll play along. Next year I'm a coed. Look out, men!"

The two guys who had been throwing the baseball were wandering by, and they kept hanging around watching Peggy's friends. The friends practically knocked themselves out, jumping around and kicking up their legs.

"What are *you* doing here?" Chels asked.

"Susie and Jennifer and I are trying out for cheerleader in September. We're practicing. There's a special team for seventh grade. You should try out, too."

I started to wish I'd sink through the asphalt to Argentina.

Peggy and her friends did a sample cheer, kicking up their legs and yelling out orders at us like real cheerleaders.

"We'll give it some thought," Chels said, "but we're probably going to be pretty busy. Vic, here, is a writer, you know. She'll probably be ace reporter on the school paper. And I have my acting, of course."

"I wouldn't trade being a cheerleader for a reporting job," Peggy said.

"You might if you were a new talent, like Vic."

That took her breath away. She looked at me. "Well, if you change your little old minds, let me know. See y'all."

29

She twitched back to her friends, pretending not to notice the guys whose eyes were practically popping out of their heads.

"What a phony," I said. "I can't believe she said 'little old minds.'"

Chelsie's voice sounded tired. "Maybe Peggy's right—if we can't lick 'em, we should join 'em. Cliques, frogs, and showers. I mean, what choice do we have?"

"When did you get to be a quitter?"

"I'm not a quitter! I just think maybe we should look into this clique business."

"Go ahead. Go be best bosom buddies with old Peggy. I don't care."

We walked a little ways.

"I'm sorry," I said.

"No biggie."

We decided to stop in and see Chelsie's grandma. One thing about Grandma Warden: you can pop in on her day or night, and she'll always be glad to see you. Thrilled, in fact.

Grandma didn't answer when we buzzed. Chels yelled through the door. For one horrible second, she sounded like a cheerleader.

We didn't hear any of the usual sounds—slippers shuffling around, chains being unbolted.

Finally Chelsie got out her key. Chels is the only person who has an extra key to Grandma's apartment, to be used only in emergencies. My heart was pumping hard, and Chelsie's fingers shook as she tried to fit the key in the lock.

Grandma Warden swung open the door. Her hair, a soft silver-white, was flat on one side as though she'd been sleeping on it.

"Didn't you *hear* us, Grandma? We practically pounded down the door." Chels sounded irritated.

"Well, give a body time to answer it," said Grandma. "Don't get into a bundle, darling grand-daughter. Hello, Victoria. Are you going to yell at me, too?"

"I just came for coffee."

"Well, let's put the pot on. Follow me."

The kitchen faces the alley, and it was dingy as always. Grandma pulled the chain over the sink, and it burst into light.

"There. That's cheery."

Grandma Warden has a way with coffee, un-matched even by my dad. Because of her, I am a coffee drinker from way back. Not that I like the taste. It's awful, if you want to know the truth. But the smell gets to me. Chels and I squeezed into chairs at the table.

"Sugar and cream, mesdemoiselles?" Grandma asked.

"Cream and sugar for me," I said. "Heavy on the sugar."

"Me, too." said Chels.

"That'll be five cents additional."

It was the old routine. Once the pot was perking full steam, Grandma joined us at the table.

31

"What brings you two calling? I thought sure you'd be out tasting the joys of summer."

"We were," I explained. "But it got too depressing. Peggy Hiltshire."

Chels shot me a glance, but I ignored it.

"Just as well," said Grandma. "I was in need of company. Beatrice is on vacation, and the building isn't quite the same without Beatrice."

Beatrice is the toy apricot poodle who belongs to Mrs. Gaston in the apartment next door. Grandma likes Beatrice a lot. Mrs. Gaston she could take or leave. "Too much opinion," she says.

"What about Mr. Wilkes?" asked Chels, with a wicked grin. She can be a real tease.

Grandma gave her a cool look. "If you're hinting about a romance, forget it. We're good friends."

"He brings you flowers," Chels accused, pointing at a glass vase of peachy pink roses.

"Certainly he does. I take him banana nut bread. Friends do things like that for each other." She grinned at us. "You two are at an age where you don't believe in that kind of friendship. But just because you don't, doesn't mean it doesn't exist."

Chels winked at me, and Grandma smacked her hand lightly.

"Anyway, I'm too old." Grandma's mouth pulled into a lopsided smile. "Even if he were sweetheart material, I'm too old for nonsense."

You can see why someone would want to hang around. I mean, for an older lady she's pretty classy. How many old ladies do you know whose eyes are the color of a Perrier bottle? She got up to pour three coffees in pink Depression glass cups. She can move quickly on those skinny legs, and I hardly even notice her limp anymore, which she's had since the stroke.

"Believe it or not, at my age those things sometimes don't matter so much. Other things do. Granddaughters. Your health. Your home."

Chels and I sneaked looks across the table at the mention of "home."

"Oh, stop, you two. Anyone ever mentions The Incident, and you get goat eyed. It wasn't so bad. I'm back home again, aren't I?"

It was bad. Last year Mr. and Mrs. Bixler wanted Grandma to move to a nursing home. Anyone who'd had a stroke had no business living alone, they said. Grandma spent one night in the home, but she packed her bags and came back the very next morning. She said it was too depressing. Mrs. Bixler was pretty upset, according to Chelsie. Now I don't think Mrs. Bixler and Grandma are even on speaking terms.

"No grudges, mesdesmoiselles. They're point-less." She took a sip, and then set her cup down hard. "I'm feeling a little tired. I've been feeling tired quite a bit lately."

"Did you go to the doctor?"

"What do doctors know? I just need a little rest."

"I think you should talk to your doctor," said

33

Chels doubtfully. "You shouldn't fool around when it comes to your health. That's a theory of mine."

"Don't nag. You're the granddaughter, remember?" Grandma Warden is always reminding Chels that she's the granddaughter.

"I'll make you lunch," I said. "I'm great with tossed salads."

"Victoria, that's kind, but I'm most in the mood for a nap. Help yourselves to a snack, if you like."

"We should go," Chels decided for us, even though I was sort of hungry.

In the elevator on the way down, Chels cracked her knuckles, which she only does when she's extremely nervous. "I didn't want to say it, but she looks terrible."

"Maybe we should tell your folks."

"That's one of your worst ideas, yet, Victoria Hope Mahoney. Mom already thinks Grandma belongs in a rest home. This would be all she'd need to convince her once and for all. I want your solemn, solemn promise that you won't tell a soul about this."

"But what if she's really sick? She didn't look that great to me either, if you want my opinion."

"She needs a little sleep, like she said. Peace and quiet."

Once Chels makes up her mind about something, there's almost no changing it. You might as well not even try. Chelsie Bixler and her grandmother are a lot alike.

5

When summer finally rolls into Minnesota, Mom switches into her cleanup mood.

She's normal the rest of the year, but practically the day after school lets out the weeds in the backyard start driving her crazy. The shrubs need trimming. There's a fraction of caulk missing around the window frame.

"Why bother with details when our house is painted spinach green?" I asked logically, digging dirt out from under my fingernails after getting every last crabgrass root out of the garden.

"We'll get to the house one day. Then all these other tasks will be taken care of." She stood looking around, hands on her hips and a determined look on her face. There were two round patches of mud on her knees. "Why don't you weed the lawn now?"

I groaned.

"But don't pull the clover. I think it makes a lawn look inviting, don't you? I hate an overmanicured yard."

I spent that whole day working on the yard, occasionally stopping to have dirt clod fights with Matthew. I didn't mind it as much as I pretended. The grass was cool, and the whole yard was shaded by the neighbors' giant cottonwood tree. The Johnstons may have the tree trunk on their property, but practically all the branches hang over into our backyard. The Johnstons probably bake all summer.

That night we picnicked out back. I spread the blue blanket, Mom carried out iced tea, and Dad was in charge of the food. Teeny grasshopper babies jumped out of his path as he came striding through the grass carrying seed-freckled watermelon wedges and burgers piled on a plate. It wasn't such a bad way to spend a summer.

Afterwards, Mom and Dad played chess on the blanket while Matthew and I kept Bullrush from catching robins.

"How'd you like to take a writing class?" Mom called to me. She must have had a lot of time to kill while Dad looked over the pieces, because she was reading a brochure.

"Me?" I asked. "*Me?* I'm just a beginner."

"I happen to think you've got great potential."

"Moms always think their kids have great potential. You wouldn't be *normal* if you didn't think I have great potential."

"Did it ever occur to you," Dad said, "that we might think you have great potential because you have great potential?"

"Oh, Dad."

"Boy, it would be great if you were a little more self-confident. Can't you try to appreciate yourself more?"

Mom kept at it. "Why not try it? Only two mornings a week. It's at the junior high school, so it'll be convenient."

"Keats?" I asked in the dramatic voice I learned from Chels.

"Of course," said Mom, puzzled. "Where else?"

"I'm not ready! I'll barely be ready for Keats in September, let alone for summer school!"

"As usual," Dad said, hunching closer to the pieces, "you've lost me. What's the scoop about Keats?" He licked two fingers, reached for a knight, and changed his mind.

I flopped down on my back, and Bullrush took the opportunity to climb on top of me. His fat sides puffed in and out with every purr. I picked cat hair off my tongue.

"I am absolutely *dreading* junior high, Dad. Peggy Hiltshire told me all the gory details."

"Who *is* this Peggy Hiltshire character? She's

certainly become a favorite topic of conversation around here."

"I know all about gym class showers," I said darkly. Then I realized that the neighbors could probably hear all of this loud and clear. I lowered my voice. "You could have warned me."

"Sorry," said Mom, "I didn't think it would be a big deal. I should have realized."

"You'll get used to it," Dad said. "Everyone does."

"I'll never get used to it!"

"Do you know what I'm going to say, Vickie?" he asked.

"Of course I do. Pray, pray, pray!"

"Well, why not? I suppose the Lord cares about gym class showers."

It would make a good experiment. A test. Maybe if I prayed hard enough, long enough—

Mom tossed the brochure to me. "In the meantime, why don't you take the class, Honey? Then when you're a famous author with books on the best-seller list, you can support me. I may grow old waiting for your father to make his next move."

Dad gave her a fake karate chop on her bare leg. "Don't rush me, don't rush me."

"I'll take the class," I said.

"This is Double Agent Slim, Gorgeous, and Intellectual," Chels said when she called later.

"I'm taking a summer writing class at Keats," I

interrupted. This was important. A genuine news flash.

"Gutsy," she said, whistling. "Very gutsy. You're a true inspiration to me, Victoria Hope Mahoney. I sure wouldn't have the nerve."

"At least I don't have to worry about showers yet," I said. Maybe later I'd tell her about my plans to pray.

"Not to change the subject or anything, but you didn't tell anyone about Grandma, did you?" Her voice was *full* of suspicion.

"Of *course* I didn't tell anyone about Grandma." I stretched the kitchen phone cord around the corner, trying to attract as little attention as possible. There is almost no such thing as privacy in our house, and I have found that it is very hard to be angry when you have to practically whisper. "What do you think I am, some kind of jerk?"

"All right, all right. Don't get huffy. I'm *worried* about her, that's all. She didn't seem too spunky."

That was for sure.

"Chels?"

"Yeah?"

"I'll pray for her."

"Yeah, okay, thanks." Chels's voice got all funny. Religion and praying and stuff embarrass Chels. The Bixlers don't pray or go to church. One time they invited me to dinner, and I was the only one at the table who bowed my head to pray. It made me feel sorry for them. But the look that Mrs. Bixler shot across the table gave me the feeling that she felt sorry for *me*.

"Someone's coming," Chels said, in a panicky whisper. "I'll call you back when the coast is clear. Over and out."

Even though Chels has a private phone in her bedroom, she has to be careful what people over-hear. She almost died the time her dad heard her tell me what fabulous thing Jeffrey Rine had said to her by the drinking fountain one day.

I went up to my room and got out my writing to look it over. I mean, when your mom thinks you have a future as one of America's greatest writers, maybe she knows something you don't know.

I keep my writing in a private of most private desk drawers. Poems, mostly, about my thoughts on things. All very personal.

Once I let Chels read some of them.

"These are good," she said, whistling. " I *really* like this one called 'i walked alone without my love.' It reminds me of e.e. cummings."

e.e. cummings doesn't use commas or periods or capital letters, either. e.e. cummings was one of Ms. Runebach's favorite poets.

"Except what do you know about love? You've never even been on a date."

"Writer's instinct."

"Oh." Chels nodded and looked at me with real respect.

That's what I like about Chels. Tell her something serious, and she doesn't laugh in your face.

I read over a lot of my old stuff, but I still couldn't tell whether it was any good or not. Maybe the writing class *was* a good idea. Maybe I'd finally find out whether I should keep sweating out poems or become an auto mechanic or something.

That night I put in a good word for Grandma Warden during my prayer. I pointed out that she was pretty much the only grandmother I've got. I don't count Grandma Shippley, since she lives up north, wears long dangly earrings, and never writes.

I also mentioned that I would appreciate it if I wasn't considered a nerd when I hit seventh grade.

6

I put on a T-shirt and some old jeans for my first day of writing class.

"It's the big day," Dad said, meeting me in the hallway. Then he took a good look. "Why the casual attire?"

"There's nothing worse than being overdressed. I'm not taking any chances."

"Are you sure, Vickie?"

"Don't worry, Dad," I said quickly, heading an argument off at the pass. "I know what I'm doing."

"Well, then, get going! You'll be late!"

I took off.

By the time I got to the school, I knew I was making a huge mistake. I felt dizzy, like I'd just gotten off the Tilt-O-Whirl at Como Park. Grandma Warden had given me some advice, and I tried saying it to myself over and over: "Remember who you are and hold your head up." I held my head up and pulled open the heavy door.

As soon as I got inside, the panic let up a little. Maybe it was the echoing emptiness of the halls. Maybe it was smell of the lunchroom. No matter what you do, you can't get rid of that old hot-lunch smell. If junior high was supposed to be so different from elementary, how come it *smelled* the same?

My shoes clattered on the linoleum, so I walked more softly, looking for the right room: 107, 105, 103. . . . There it was—room 101.

I stared at the three other kids sitting at desks. They stared at me.

"Come on in," said the girl in the front row. "The more the merrier." She had wild red lips.

The desk was just a flat, yellow top held up by shiny, tubed legs. No insides for stashing stuff. No place even to put a pencil. It felt weird. It felt somewhat mature. I liked it.

We were all trying not to look at each other, but I got a peek at the two guys in the class. They sat slouched in their chairs.

"Hey." I jumped when the girl with the flashy lips whacked my arm. "Got a mirror?" Her hand was cupped over one eye, and she was squinting at me with the other.

All I had was this dumb one I've been lugging

around since I was a kid. It has a stupid cartoon on the back that says, "Mary had a little lamb."

I wrote an imaginary note to myself: *Get new mirror.*

"Thanks," said the girl, after fiddling with her eye awhile. "Contacts."

"Your parents let you wear contacts?"

"Oh, sure. On account of I'm fairly mature."

"Do they hurt?"

"Nah. I just jabbed myself with my mascara. Happens occasionally. Nothing to get excited about." She blinked a couple of times, and there was so much lavender on her eyelids you wouldn't have believed it. Chelsie would have loved it.

I was just going to ask her where she bought her eye shadow, when the door squeaked open, and a man in a gray sweat shirt and jeans came in. His dark beard and moustache were so short they looked more like shadows on his face. He had a round bald spot on the top of his head.

"I'm Mr. Harrison, but you can call me Ted."

He made us go around the room and tell about ourselves. The girl with contacts said her real name was Betsy Bonnoff, but we could call her by her pen name: Melody McClure. She was writing a novel. So far, she was on page sixteen.

The blond guy got up. He had a buzz cut, but he kept running his hand over it like he was brushing back long hair. Mr. Harrison made him take off his sunglasses. The guy said he was from New York, but he was visiting his cousin during the summer. His name was Calvin.

"My name's Peter." The guy with the black hair looked at his shoes. Then he pulled a pair of glasses out of his pocket and put them on. "I think glasses make writers look smarter."

The rest of us laughed, and the room felt less tight, less like it was pulling at its seams. Peter, I noticed, had a nice smile.

My turn. "I'm Victoria Hope Mahoney," I said, and my voice rang in my ears. I have a habit of talking too loudly when I'm nervous.

Ted leaned against his desk, twisting the ends of his moustache. "Tell us something interesting about yourself, Victoria."

I couldn't think of a thing. *Polar bear in a snowstorm,* my mind said idiotically, over and over.

"Hobbies?" said the teacher. "Interests? Pastimes?"

The class made little snickering sounds.

"I think—and I'm sure the class will concur with me on this one—that one very interesting thing about you is that you can't think of one very interesting thing about yourself. That is truly amazing. Eh, class?" Everyone clapped as I slithered back into my seat. Ted clapped, too, and gave me a very nice smile. I'm sure my face was the color of Melody's lipstick, but his smile made me want to smile a little, too. Can't take yourself too seriously, as Dad would say.

"Let's start with some writing exercises. Write what you wish you could be."

Rich, I wrote. Then I scratched that out and put: *Eighth grader*. It was supposed to be a joke. Also, I was too nervous to think of anything else. Luckily, Ted didn't make us hand those in.

"Write about someone you respect."

I looked at my paper, took a deep breath, and started to write:

Grandma Warden is a very classy lady who doesn't dye her hair. Her real name is Sapphira and she has hair the color of moth wings, very soft and white. I asked her once why she doesn't dye it, and she said because white hair is who she is, Mr. Wilkes or no Mr. Wilkes. She says artifice in anyone is superfluous. I love her more than staying up late, or peanut clusters. And she's not even my own grandma.

"Mind if I read them aloud?" Ignoring our groans, Ted collected the papers and went ahead. I could hardly hear him, my heart was thudding so loud. "Grandma Warden is a very classy lady—"

I thought I would pass out. Fortunately I didn't, so I tried to concentrate on my work. It didn't sound half bad when Ted read it.

"This is *good*, Vickie. There's texture. There's honesty. There's characterization."

I finally looked up. Ted was looking right into my eyes. His seemed to be saying, "Believe me! I'm telling you the truth!"

46

I eased back against my chair, feeling tension go out of my shoulders and back. This was fun.

When we were ready to leave, Ted shook our hands and said, "Your assignment for this class will be to become more confident as writers. Keeping a journal of your experiences is a good idea. You won't have to read them to the class, so don't code your messages or anything. Try to be honest and be yourself."

"This will be fun," Melody said, blinking at me with red and blurry eyes.

"See ya," said Calvin, passing my desk.

"Yeah, see ya," Peter said, not looking me in the eye.

I walked through the dim halls, past rows and rows of lockers and locked classroom doors. I was still smiling when I got home.

7

"And *then* what?" Chels asked. "Did you dazzle
'em with your wild creativity?"

We were lying out in our bathing suits in Bixlers'
backyard. Chels had rubbed about a gallon of
suntan oil over herself. She has tended to overdo it
since her *magna* burn at the state fair last summer.

"The teacher read what I wrote about Grandma."

"Really? Were you a hit?"

"He said I was honest and textured."

"You're kidding! Vic, you're on your way to
stardom. I can just see you on the Johnny Carson
show. I hope you'll remember who stuck by you
during your climb to the top."

I giggled.

Chels stretched and rolled onto her back. "Was *Peter* impressed?"

"You're not going to bug me about him all the time, are you? Because if you are—"

"I always told you about Jeffrey Rine."

"There wasn't much to tell about Jeffrey Rine." Then, seeing her face, I added, "Although there was definitely chemistry between you."

"The spark becomes a flame," Chels said mysteriously.

I was quiet for a while. Chelsie slid her sunglasses down to the end of her nose. "I've been thinking. Want to hear my great plan for next year? We get *excused* from gym class. Very legit."

"Excused for the *whole year?*"

"It's a cinch. Doctors' permission slips. 'To whom it may concern. Please excuse Chelsie Bixler from gym class this year. She has athlete's foot.' "

"But you don't *have* athlete's foot."

"Do you think they're gonna check? No way! Gross."

"But we'd have to go to the doctor to get the permission slips."

"I forgot about that. And you know how I feel about doctors. I hate them almost as much as I hate gym showers."

I was sweating like crazy, but it was worth it. I'll do anything for a tan. Fortunately, I practically get tan *thinking* about sun.

"Did you hear I have a baby-sitting job?"

Chelsie sat up, whipping off her glasses.

"You do? Who for?"

"The Johnstons. You don't know them. They live next door."

"Boy. I wish I had a baby-sitting job."

"You can have mine, except I have to keep it. My folks said I have to chip in for the writing class."

"You're kidding. My parents would love it if I took a class this summer. They'd pay the way, believe me."

Mrs. Bixler came out with two glasses of fresh lemonade, *from real lemons*. I said thank you as sincerely as I could. Mrs. Bixler just smiled like she was one million miles away. Maybe it was my imagination. And it probably didn't help that I couldn't stop staring at her clothes. Her blouse had *sequins* on it. Oh, boy. My mom would die before she wore sequins. Sequins are definitely not her style. Mrs. Bixler went back in the house.

We soaked up some more rays without talking for a while, until Chels switched to her stomach and said sleepily, "I wonder what old Ms. Runebach is doing. I wonder if she has a personal life during the summer."

"Of course she has a personal life. She's human, isn't she?" But it was kind of a weird thought. I have always had this problem believing that really classy people do normal things, and Ms. Runebach is a very classy person—probably the classiest person we know. For instance, does a

50

person like Ms. Runebach blow her nose? I, for one, have never seen Ms. Runebach blow her nose.

"All I know," said Chels, "is if I were her I'd probably be on a date every night."

"What are *you* worried about?" I asked, just a little on the snotty side. "All you have to do is stand next to a roller rink."

"Oh, brother. You're not going to start that again, are you?"

Once I invited Chelsie to go roller-skating with my Sunday school class, and it was terrible. Halfway through the night, the DJ got the bright idea to have a Snowball Skate. That's when all the girls line up on one side of the rink, and the boys line up on the other. When the music starts, one couple starts skating around. Then they break up and each picks another partner. And so on. You're supposed to stand there like an idiot until you get picked to skate with some bozo. The Snowball Skate was invented by someone really sick.

I went along with it for a while, but it was torture, pure torture. Just when it seemed that someone was finally skating toward me, he'd pick someone else. Guys. They're all so hung up on getting the cutest girl in the world that they won't touch anyone else with a ten-foot pole. Most guys I know are not especially cute themselves. Most of them are real slobs.

Chelsie skated with Chet Mulligan, the tallest guy in the Sunday school. I watched her roll

51

around and around that rink with her hair breezing out behind her, and there was this dizzy feeling in my head. It was a really strange feeling, not a good feeling at all. It got even worse when Chet gave her his great smile, all teeth. The Snowball Skate is bad enough without your best friend practically being the Snowball Queen.

Chels gave me a squirt with the water bottle, waking me up out of my daydream-nightmare.

"If you hadn't chickened out and gone to the snack bar," she was saying, "you would have gotten picked."

I closed my eyes and let the sun beat down. Maybe it would bake the memory of the Snowball Skate right out of my brain. "Do we *have* to talk about it?"

"Anyway," she said, her voice muffled because her face was smashed into her beach towel, "maybe you'll get to be friends with someone really debonair in writing class."

Fat chance.

8

I was writing in my journal when Dad called me downstairs to help unpack groceries. Matthew stood on a kitchen chair and did Mr. T impersonations while I helped. It is my opinion that Matthew is extremely spoiled, being the last baby and all. Some kids I know are *never* allowed to stand on the furniture.

"You didn't get Banana Flakes, Dad," Matthew pointed out as we got to the last bag. "I wanted Banana Flakes."

"Look here, Matthew, old boy. How about these delicious Bran Squares?"

"Bran Squares?" My brother's eyes got big.

"I'm trying to cut back on luxuries," Dad said,

pulling out the *second* box of macaroni and cheese. "Banana Flakes are luxuries. But you haven't lived till you've tried my Econo-Beans-and-Franks."

I didn't think this was funny.

"Is that on tonight's menu?" I asked. "If it is, I think Chelsie might want me to eat over at her house."

Dad didn't think I was funny, either. "No, Smarty. Tonight's chicken. I thought the three of us could whip up something special, this being Mom's first day at Willowood."

Food is a very big tradition in our house. We went to work on a chicken, peeling its slimy old skin.

"Dad," I said, "can't we have *any* luxuries anymore?"

"Oh, come on. Things aren't that desperate. We'll tighten up the proverbial belt a bit, but we'll be fine."

Matthew dragged cold chicken skin across my neck. I screamed.

"How can we tighten up?" I demanded. "What luxuries did we ever have?" For as long as I can remember, my family has been on a budget. When you're a little kid, stuff like that doesn't matter. But last year, when everyone else had this very specific kind of jeans, I had to get mine at Valu-Plus. I would rather die than tell anyone I bought jeans at Valu-Plus. I never even told Chels.

"*What* luxuries?" I said again, a little louder.

"Nonessentials. Vacations. Eating out." Dad paused. "New school clothes."

"Da-ad!" I howled.

I put down the chicken drumstick I was working on. In all my life I hadn't had a more depressing couple of days.

"Do-not-whine," said Dad darkly, continuing to cut up chicken parts.

I took a deep breath. "I just have one thing to say." My voice was very calm.

"What?"

"I'm going into seventh grade next year."

"So?" Dad looked at me as though he didn't get the joke.

"So school clothes aren't a luxury in seventh grade. They're a necessity."

"You *have* nice clothes."

"Dad, they're awful." I bit down on my lip and grabbed at the chicken again.

"I wanted roller skates," Matthew said. "I thought for sure this summer you'd get me roller skates."

For a long time we worked silently. The Mahoney brigade. I had this tight feeling in my chest. Life gets more complicated, the older you get.

Suddenly Dad snapped his fingers and pointed to me with a great smile. "Hey! You could earn some money. You know, odd jobs. Mr. Lee asked me if I knew anyone around the neighborhood doing odd jobs—weed pulling, lawn mowing, that sort of thing. Might be good for you."

Let me just say here and now that the idea didn't thrill me.

"I could pull weeds," piped up Matthew. "I am the greatest weed puller ever."

"I bet you are. Well, at least you can think about it, eh, Vickie? This whole thing was a pretty big decision for your mother and me, and I recall that you had a say, too. Try to be tolerant—for our sakes. Think of the good your mother is doing over at Willowood."

I hated Willowood. And everyone in it.

9

I let the phone ring ten times before I hung up.

"Isn't Chelsie home?" Matthew asked, disappointed. He was hoping she would be coming over. He had more acrobatics to show her.

"Maybe I dialed wrong."

I let it ring *eleven* times.

Matthew sighed. "Do *you* want to play?"

"Go over to Kevin's."

"He's at piano lessons."

"Go over to Jessica's."

"I hate Jessica."

"Well, I'm going to look for Chelsie. And you're not invited."

He opened his mouth.

"If you scream," I said quickly, "a green and black pox will infect your body."

Matthew shut his mouth and went out to the garden to tell Dad about the pox.

I checked all our old spots. I even went over to Keats. Chelsie wasn't anywhere. I headed over to Grandma's.

It took her a long time to come to the door.

"Hi, Grandma. Is Chelsie here?"

"Who?" she asked, wrinkling her wrinkled face.

"*Chelsie.* Are you okay, Grandma?"

"I—I better sit down."

After a bit she said she felt better. "Whom did you say you wanted to see?"

"I've looked everywhere for Chelsie. I thought she might be here."

"Oh, *Chelsie.*" She said it as though she hadn't heard me the first time. "No, I haven't seen her. She's been making herself scarce lately."

She cooked up a batch of her famous coffee. "Cream and sugar, mademoiselle?" she asked.

We went into the living room and headed for our favorite chairs. Mine is the red velvet one that's about a hundred years old. You have to be careful not to sit too hard; the springs tend to sag. Grandma set her cup on the arm of the loveseat.

"The best seat in the house," she said, tucking her skirt around her legs, and of course not spilling coffee. "Best all-around view of the city. I sure love the high-rise life."

We sipped our coffee for a while, and the clock in the hallway thumped along like a heartbeat. I thought about Mrs. Bixler, and wondered if she was ever sorry she couldn't come over and drink coffee with her mother. The morning sunlight slanted through the window and lit up Grandma's face as she blew into her cup.

"You look pensive, Victoria."

"I was thinking about Mrs. Bixler. Your daughter."

"Oh, Amanda. She's in a snit, but she'll snap out of it. She's just being troublesome." But her face darkened, and she got serious. "I pray for her every night."

"I will, too!"

"Wonderful. With God's help, how long can this silent treatment last?"

I wasn't sure, considering how Mrs. Bixler can be sometimes. I didn't say this to Grandma.

"While you're at it, Grandma, you could pray about her and me. I don't think she likes me much either."

"Oh, dear. Do you think it's money?"

"I *know* it's money. I asked Mom and Dad if we could please move to The Circle, but they said no."

"Move to The Circle! That's ridiculous!"

"But, if we did, maybe—"

"Let's not mince words, Victoria. Your parents are just this side of poor. They're not likely to be moving anywhere."

She was right. It hit me right between the eyes.

"And you're jim-dandy just the way you are. Don't forget that. The sooner you stop worrying about *things*, the better off you'll be. None of this phony baloney put-on stuff. You take your Mr. Wilkes, for instance. He doesn't have two coins to rub together, but he's very down to earth."

She lifted her chin and gave me a very pink look. It occurred to me that maybe she hadn't been telling us the whole truth about old Mr. Wilkes the other day. I opened my mouth to ask her more, but she interrupted: "Tell me about your writing class."

"I've only been once so far, but I'm working on a special poetry project."

"A sonnet?" she guessed. "Sestina? Villanelle?"

"Just a regular poem." It was too early to let the cat out of the bag.

"I'm proud to know a real poet. People depend on poets, you know. We all see the world in different ways, but poets can say things as no one else says them."

I'd never thought of that before.

"Just be yourself; that's my advice. Be yourself and you can't go wrong."

Twenty-one floors below, a siren shrieked. I shivered. It was almost noon, so I said I had to go. Dad would be leaving for work, and I had to look after Matthew.

"If Chelsie shows up, tell her I'm looking for her. I want her to come over this afternoon."

"I hope I see her," Grandma said, seeing me to the door. "She certainly has been scarce."

Matthew was waiting for me on the front steps. "Chelsie's been calling and calling. Maybe she can come over now."

I called her up.

"Where have you *been*?" she asked.

"Where have *you* been?" I asked.

"You won't believe it. Peggy Hiltshire came over this morning. She wanted me to come with her to buy her gym suit, but they weren't out yet."

I didn't say anything, so Chels went right on.

"We tried on every perfume at the cosmetic counter. Do I smell!"

"I'll talk to you tonight," I said. "Dad's leaving for work, and I've got to play a game with Matthew." I didn't invite her over.

Matthew looked at me when I hung up. "Want to play a game?" he asked hopefully.

10

I prayed a very selfish prayer that night. I have been known to do that occasionally.

God, I want to be popular. I want to have lots of friends. And please let my hair grow out.

Then I got into bed and went right to sleep. It didn't even hit me that it was a selfish prayer until the next day, when I remembered that I had promised Grandma to pray for Mrs. Bixler. I prayed while I was making my bed, but it wasn't the same.

"Hey," said Mom, appearing at my door. "Want to go out today? Do something exotic?"

"How come?" Usually on Saturdays parents like to do things like clean the garage or weed the lawn.

"A small thank-you for watching Matthew while Dad and I are at work. And for being responsible, and for baby-sitting all on your own. Dad's going to play with him this afternoon, so we can do something special."

I immediately got this feeling in my stomach like too much hot dogs, peanuts, and fudge ice cream at a baseball game. I didn't have the heart to tell her I usually think Matthew is sort of a jerk. And sometimes I treat him like it, too.

"Well? Do you have any ideas?"

"Pizza!"

"*Pizza*? Who do you think you're talking to, your father? We'll get pocket sandwiches at the Veggie Cafe."

It sounded great. I was ready to go, but I put the old Vickie Mahoney finishing touches on my bed anyway. I may not be the world's tidiest person, but I can make a smooth bed.

Mom was very funny at the restaurant. She was in a great mood, and by dessert I had her talked into a yogurt sundae with carob chips. I had the one hundred percent natural Rocky Road with jimmies.

Later, I told Chelsie all about it.

"That sounds great," she said. "Your mom is spectacular. She's very colorful."

"What did *you* do today?"

She brightened up. "Peggy came over again."

"Really?" It was amazing, it really was, how I made my voice sound so normal. You would never have known that Peggy going to Chelsie's house bugged me.

"She thinks she can get me into glee club. She knows the music instructor on account of her sister being in eighth grade and all."

"I don't sing."

"I said me, not you, didn't I? She thinks she can get *me* into glee club."

"I didn't know you liked to sing, either."

"In junior high school it's important to experience a variety of things. It just so happens that a lot of people would jump at the chance to sing in the glee club."

She started yodeling, then switched to opera. By the time she got to country-western I was singing along and practically falling off the phone. Dad walked by and gave me a look with eyebrows in it.

"Chelsie," I said, "you know what? You're going to think I'm jealous or something, but I know for a fact that Peggy would never in one million years come to my house."

"She's shy."

"Peggy Hiltshire is not shy!"

"I've known her longer than you, Vic; she has to warm up to people. But if she can get me into glee club, I think I should at least be friendly to her."

"Next thing you'll be talking about getting into the right cliques."

"Oh, forget it, Vic. Your poor self-image is showing again."

64

I thought she'd be really mad at me, but she snapped out of it. "Have you been working on any hot new stuff for writing class?"

"A poem," I said. "For Grandma. But it's a surprise. Last time Ted said we should write about what we know, so I'm writing a poem in honor of Grandma."

"Vic, that's deeply moving. Let's show it to Grandma right away. She'll love it."

"Not yet! It's not ready. I'm not showing anything until it's done."

"Victoria, you can show it to Grandma, can't you? She'll get a kick out of it."

I was silent.

"Victoria, sometimes you drive me crazy."

11

"I don't believe my eyes," Mom said, coming into the family room. Matthew and I were playing Weasel Race, a very stupid board game he got for Christmas last year. "My children, cooperating? Sharing? Getting along?"

Mom can be very sarcastic sometimes.

"Someone who is going into the seventh grade should be able to get along with her one and only brother," I told her in a very mature voice.

"Same here," said Matthew.

Mom leaned over and kissed Matthew and then me. She smelled delicious. "All I can say is it's music to my ears to hear you two in here quietly playing a game. You don't know."

66

Matthew blew on the spinner, shook it behind his back, and turned it over and over for good luck—a habit of his that nearly drives me crazy.

"While you're in a convivial mood, I'll give you something to think about," Mom continued, sitting down on the couch and folding her arms for one of her talks. Always beware when a parent folds her arms. "I think you should both visit Willowood sometime. I've met an awful lot of lonely people over there. They'd appreciate an afternoon with some spunky little kids."

Spunky little kids! I groaned.

"I'm awfully busy these days," I said. "I'm helping the neighbors with yard work. Not to mention baby-sitting, my writing class—"

"I'm awfully busy these days, too," said Matthew with dignity.

Mom sighed. She looked pretty disappointed. "Matthew, I don't want you coming over alone if Vickie can't walk with you. Some other time, then." She headed off to work.

"After this," Matthew said, "want to play with my hot-rod cars?"

"Don't get used to this, Matthew. It's not like I don't have other things to do. In fact, I've got a very important call to make this very instant."

Chels answered on the first ring.

"Hi."

"Hi."

"I'm going to class this morning."

67

"Well, this time find out what kind of makeup Melody uses."

We have agreed that it's time to start discussing makeup with our parents.

"I will. Have you talked to your mother?"

"Sort of. It didn't go so hot. You know it'll take a miracle to convince my mom. Remember the nylons?"

Last summer we needed permission to wear nylons. My parents finally said okay, but Chel's dad said no way was any eleven-year-old of his going to wear nylons. That killed me. Chels is at least six months older than me, and I thought she'd get permission easy. After that, Chels stopped rubbing in the six-months-older thing. She also stopped wearing dresses.

"I better go," I told her. "It's almost time for class, and if I get there early, I can watch her put on makeup before. I don't think she'd mind."

"I want a full report."

"Agent Eye Shadow, over and out."

12

"Good morning, future poets and playwrights," Ted announced as we came into the classroom. "It's good to see you all. Not one dropout. Good. Let's get to work."

We wrote a bunch of haiku, which I personally found very boring. Limericks don't thrill me, either, if you want to know the truth.

"Now, I want you to write a short poem on something that means a lot to you."

"Like money?" Calvin asked.

Ted smiled.

Melody's hand shot up. "Can we write about love?"

Everyone snickered.

Ted looked puzzled. "Sure," he said. "If you have something to say."

I tried to write about love. I fooled around with words like *fiery* and *fervent*. But all I knew about love is that Ms. Runebach was probably on a date every night. Then I decided my poem about Grandma qualified. I pulled it out and took a look. Pretty rough.

At the end of class Ted wanted us to read our stuff aloud.

I was the very last. I cleared my throat. "This is no good, but—"

Ted jumped out of his chair. "Never start a poem that way! Victoria, you're a good writer, but you need confidence. Now start again."

"The name of my poem—" I said, blushing about a hundred shades of red.

Old Peter, the guy with the glasses, had his arms behind his head, and a little cat smile. But maybe I dreamed that part.

When I finished, Melody spoke right up. "I think that poem came from her heart. There was nothing phony about it."

"Nice idea," Cal said.

I probably didn't hear another word the rest of the class. In fact, I was in a kind of daze, which is why I was still sitting in my desk at break when Pauline Barney stuck her head in the door.

Pauline is a popular girl in my grade, but she is not popular the way Peggy Hiltshire is popular. In other words, she does not act stupid around boys and snotty to people who are not popular. I think she is the most unphony popular person I know.

"Hi, Peter! Hi, Vickie. Have you heard about my pre-seventh party? I'm inviting everyone in our class. Nothing fancy, just homemade pizza. Do you think you can come? Last week of August."

I looked at Peter. He was looking at his shoes.

"Sure," I said.

"Good. Tell Chelsie, too. Absolutely everyone has to be there. You, too, Peter."

I flashed her the old Mahoney smile. She waved and left, and while I was still in the smiling mood, I sent a flasher over to Peter, too, an incredibly brave thing to do.

"I could just die. I could die of excitement," Chelsie said, when I stopped by her house to tell her the news. She closed the bedroom door for privacy. "How did Pauline sound? What was she wearing?"

"Something ungrubby. Pauline is very careful about that sort of thing."

"I can't stand it. I may have a nervous breakdown. I don't know how I'll act or what I'll say. We'd better practice."

The trouble with having an actor for a best friend is she's always wanting to act things out. Writers are not into acting.

"I'll be a boy at Pauline's party," Chelsie said.

"Oh, all right, but you'll have to pretend I'm

71

wearing all new clothes. They're fabulous clothes."

"Got ya."

"And my hair is down to my waist."

"Wait a minute. You can't just make things up."

"Just *pretend*. My hair will definitely be a little longer by then."

"Okay, okay."

I rapped an imaginary door.

"Hi, Victoria," said Chels, opening the door, and talking in a deep voice. "I'm Peter. Come on in."

"Hello, Peter. You can call me Vic. All my friends call me Vic."

Chels exploded with laughter. "I'm madly in love with you, Old Vic! Come away with me. Come share my locker!"

I pushed her away. "You wrecked the mood."

"I'm in a great mood!" She doubled over, clutching her stomach. "I'm dying!"

My face burned. "I'm not going to do this if you won't be serious."

"All my friends call me Vic!" she yelped. She sprawled on the bed and kicked. Finally she got up, wiping tears out of her eyes.

"I'm sorry," she croaked. "I got carried away. I'm sorry, I really am. Please, Vic? I'll be good."

Usually it's hard for me to stay mad at her, but this time I shook off the hand she put on my arm.

"I'll be good," she promised again.

"You'd better be," I warned her.

"Okay, let's do it again. You be the guy. I'm

72

going to Pauline's party. Ring-ring!"

An idea came in a flash, and I could hardly keep from smirking as I opened a pretend door. "Yeah?"

"I'm Chelsie Bixler. I was invited to Pauline's party."

"I'm Jeffrey Rine."

"Oh!" She said it so surprised, it was almost like she had forgotten it was me and not really Jeffrey. I have heard that this happens with really good actors. "Hi, Jeff. Can I come in?"

"Let's see your invitation."

She held up her make-believe invite. "Can I come in now?"

"No."

"Why not?" she asked.

"Because." I said the next part very slowly. "People with braces are not allowed at Pauline's parties. Braces make us sick."

Right away I was sorry I had done it. Her whole face kind of drooped.

"Real funny," she said, smiling weakly, as if it had been a joke, which it hadn't.

"Listen, Chels. I didn't mean it. I was getting you back for—"

"It's okay."

"Your braces hardly show." I was definitely making things worse. "I mean, if they really did show, I wouldn't have said it. I'm sorry."

"I'm going out," she said.

She started walking. I followed like a stupid dog.

We headed toward Goose Lake, which is right down the hill from her house. It was hot. The crickets were going crazy, hiding in the reeds. Spiky weeds stuck in my socks.

At the muddy lakeshore, Chels took off her shoes and dabbed her toes in the water. I untied my tennis shoes, and dragged off the hot socks. The water was cold and wonderful.

"Do you think it will be like that?" Chels said, out of the blue.

"What?" I hoped my voice sounded sorry.

"Junior high. Do you think the other kids will make fun of me?"

"Of course not!" I said. "They'd be crazy if they did. You're beautiful. Remember the Snowball Skate."

She didn't laugh. "I just want to be prepared. I want to know what to expect."

"I don't know," I told her. "*I* sure don't know what to expect."

"I guess I'm stuck."

"Yeah," I said. "We're stuck."

On the way home I said I was sorry about a hundred times, but Chelsie was a million miles away. It looked like I was in for the old silent treatment.

Some people can really hold a grudge.

13

A good writer will spend hours on a poem, getting it right, digging up the weeds and the crabgrass, getting dirt under her fingernails. That's what Ted says.

"Sweat a little!" His voice shouted into my brain.

I worked *hard* on my poem. Not that there was much to do otherwise, which there wasn't, unless you count baby-sitting, which I don't. Baby-sitting is something my mom would call a necessary evil. Every time the phone rang, it was another baby-sitting job.

"At your age," Dad told me, spraying icy hose water over our soaped-up car, "I would have been glad for a little spending money. Jobs are part of reality, my dear. Part of earning your own way in this world."

I *didn't* say that people like Chelsie don't have to worry about baby-sitting. It would not have pleased him.

And the worst thing was, I hadn't heard from Chelsie in a week. Loneliness was setting in.

A weird thing happened: I talked to Matthew about it. We were outside. Matthew was swinging on the gate, and I don't know why, but I just started talking to him as though he were a normal person.

"She must really be mad," I said. "I've never seen her so mad."

"Why don't you call her up and say you're sorry?"

"It's not that easy," I said.

"That's what I'd do. Just call her up and say, 'I'm sorry.' "

"Don't be dumb."

Mom and Dad were on overlapping shifts, and I wasn't going to take any funny business from him. Then I took a look at his face, and I felt sorry for being mean.

"I'm bored stiff, Matthew, old boy. Let's go over to see Chelsie's grandma."

"A grandma?" He lifted one eyebrow. He is suspicious of grandmas, probably because of our strange one.

"She's pretty nice. And she lives in an apartment

on the twenty-first floor of a high rise."

"Wow. The twenty-*first*?"

I made him put on a clean shirt and wash the orange Popsicle off his mouth. His eyes practically bugged out of his head as the elevator rose to Grandma's floor—19, 20, 21. I let him knock.

"Surprise, Grandma," I said. "That's a snappy outfit."

Her hair looked as though she'd been sleeping on it again, but her eyes sparkled when she saw me. "Greetings, mademoi— Oops, there's a monsieur here, too. Come in, come in. Who's this? a special friend?"

"My brother," I said. "Matthew."

She gave me a very shocked look. "You never told me you had a brother. Glad to meet you, Matthew."

They shook hands.

Matthew ran to the window. "Look at that! We're in the clouds!" Matthew is a very sheltered kid.

"Let's go for a walk!" I suggested. Grandma looked as though she could use a little fresh air. She went to put on her Nikes.

Matthew held her hand all the way to the park. He's an affectionate kid; I'll say that for him. The sun was so bright it made me sneeze. Grandma sneezed, too. Matthew wanted to, but he didn't.

We walked slowly. People whizzed by us on skates. A dog with big watery jowls and happy

77

brown eyes came up and snuffed my hand. It was a beautiful day. A day for poems. I walked a little ahead, so I could keep my own pace, taking long steps and missing the cracks. Matthew was chattering away, telling Grandma about his triple backwards roll or something.

"Victoria," Grandma said behind me, "I think I'd like to sit a spell. Over there, under that tree."

Matthew ran off to swing, and the two of us sat in the shade. My legs were very tan. Grandma's arms were white and thin, and when she grasped my hand I could feel the bones.

"Amanda called me this week," she said. "What do you think of that?"

"She's coming over for a visit!" I guessed.

"No, she was just calling about my electric bill. But it's a start."

"Oh."

"How about you? Have you made any headway?"

"No. In fact, I'm hardly on speaking terms with Chelsie. I made fun of her braces."

"Oh, that's serious," Grandma said, but her teeth showed in a smile. "She'll forgive you."

We let the breeze cool us and watched Matthew soar higher and higher on the swing.

"I have something to show you," I said, finally getting up the nerve. "Something I wrote. It's a poem." I unfolded the sheet and handed it to her.

"Oh, no. You read it, honey."

I didn't want to, but she was already leaning back

with her eyes closed. I cleared my throat.
"Grandma
wears smiles for jewels
is dainty as pink cups set in saucers.
She sweetens
the day with cream and sugar
and her prayers
are red balloons
that float to heaven.
Grandma says
God turns prayer to precious things.
So
when I'm low
I think of her,
and God thinks, too,
of fresh-ground coffee, sun, and roses."
Afterward, she didn't open her eyes.

"Grandma?"

"I'm just savoring it," she said. Her eyes opened. "What a lovely tribute."

"It's not very good," I said.

Grandma gave me a stern look. "You're not to say your poems aren't good. God gave you a gift, Victoria. Don't underestimate it!"

She laughed at Matthew, who was now hanging upside down on the jungle gym. "Shall we call Matthew in before he tries a triple flip? What a charming boy! I don't know why you didn't tell me about him sooner."

Wait till she gets to know him.

14

"Is someone going to answer that?" Dad asked when the phone rang for the third time. He put down his knife and fork, and looked meaningfully at me. "I would, but it's never for me."

"It's probably for Vickie," said Matthew. "Another baby-sitting job." He ducked when I aimed one at him.

"Victoria," Mom said.

I got up to answer the phone. It was Chelsie. I was so surprised at first I couldn't think of a thing to say. Fortunately, she was in a terrific mood and she talked nonstop. Finally she took a breath.

"I got my gym suit," I told her. The ugly thing. It made me sick.

"Can you come over? We can talk about school."

"Okay. After supper."

"I'll be on the deck."

Chels had on a new sophisticated top and great shorts. She looked like a million. Someone who looks like a million in shorts and a top doesn't need to worry about nylons or makeup.

"Hi," she yelled down at me. "Well? Let's see it. Did you bring it?"

I yanked the ugly navy and powder blue gym suit out of its sack.

"Great," said Chels, looking pleased, as if I had picked it out of a rack of a thousand different styles. "Here's mine."

Her suit was exactly like mine, only bigger.

"Have you tried yours on?" I asked.

"Fits great. How about you?"

"It's okay." Actually, it made me look flat and skinny. I wished I would never have to wear it.

She folded hers up like it was a cashmere sweater or something. "We're on our way. In a matter of weeks we'll be Keats freshmen."

There were footsteps on the deck stairs. I whipped around, and my eyes bugged out of my head. It was Peggy.

"Hi, Chels," said Peggy. "Oh, hi, Vickie."

Chels smiled so her braces didn't show, but she looked a little embarrassed. She had planned this whole thing. I felt my heartbeat speed up.

"What were you two talking about?" Peggy

wanted to know, using her finger to smooth out her lip gloss, which sparkled like glitter.

"Oh, school. Seventh grade," said Chels, fiddling with the button on her top. "I'm so excited."

I almost dropped through the deck.

"Just think. Keats has its own swimming pool, so we can take lessons. And I can be the star in the theatre. And you can be number-one newspaper reporter, and Peggy here will be the most popular cheerleader in the school. And best of all, we'll be elbow to elbow with loads of boys."

It was funny. They were all reasons I wanted to go to Keats. And reasons I didn't.

"Watch this," said Chels, suddenly, hopping down the steps. "Peggy taught me." She put her feet apart and her hands on her waist. Then she started jumping around like mad.

"Give me a K! Give me an E! Give me an A! Give me a T! What's it spell?!"

"Keat."

She stopped. "What?"

"Keat. You spelled Keat. It's supposed to be Keats."

Peggy laughed. "You say the funniest things."

"Give me an S! What's it spell? Keats! Keats! Yaaaaay, Keats!" She scissored her legs. "I'm gonna try out for cheerleader."

I felt like I'd been slugged.

"*You?*"

"Why not? Everyone wants to be a cheerleader."

She stretched her leg, leaning over to put her head against her knee.

"You didn't," I said. "Not until Peggy arrived on the scene."

Her face changed. "What do you know? Keep your stupid opinions to yourself."

"Really," Peggy said.

"You're only doing it because you're afraid of her!" I said. For some stupid reason I felt like bawling, really letting loose like Matthew. My eyes watered, but I ground my teeth together, staring fiercely at Chelsie and Peggy.

"You're scared," Chelsie said. "You're afraid you're not pretty enough. You're afraid you'd never make it." Her eyes were angry slits.

"I hope—" I paused, trying to think of something awful to say, something terrible and secret that only Chelsie Bixler would understand. "Your grandma can die for all I care!"

I turned, stumbling, and started running. I didn't know where I was going. I just had to get out of there.

"What did she mean by that?" I heard Peggy drawl. "What a weird thing to say."

Chelsie didn't answer.

15

"Let me in." Matthew sounded muffled behind my not only closed but locked bedroom door. "I have to tell you something."

"Go away!"

After I finally heard his footsteps clunk back down the stairs, I punched up my pillow, flopped against it, and uncapped my pen. I wrote down all the horrible things I *could* have said to make Chelsie feel even worse. I wrote them right in my journal. Snob. Creep. Two-faced jerk. She deserved them all. I wished I'd said them.

Then I got to feeling so guilty I could hardly stand it. That's the trouble with being raised a Christian. Anytime you really feel like letting somebody have it, *really* letting them have it, the old conscience steps in and makes you feel rotten.

I looked at all the things I had written, and they did not make me feel good. A drop hit the page with a tiny *smack*, spreading the ink. One tear. I set the sheet on my desk to dry and turned out the light. That drop would remind me forever what today had felt like.

It was quiet in my room, except for Bullrush purring, snuggled in the covers. I heard Mom and Dad walking around below, running water. I even heard Mom tap her toothbrush three times against the sink, the way she always does, as if nothing in the world had changed. But everything had changed. Things would never be the same.

I have a book of devotions I got for memorizing verses a couple of years ago in Vacation Bible School. A girl in Sunday school said that if you feel guilty about something, your devotions will be about lying or whatever it is you're feeling guilty about. I snapped the light back on and opened the book, just to test the theory out. The passage I put my finger on had nothing to do with Chelsie or with saying rotten things to your friends. But the whole time I was reading it, my mind was on Chelsie, my ex-best friend.

I got down on my knees. "I'm going crazy, God! I really think I'm going crazy. But Chelsie was worse than I was. You saw that, didn't you? She deserved what I said."

But the idea that I had been wrong wouldn't go away.

I prayed so long I fell asleep on my knees in the dark. Then I had to pray like crazy some more. "Forgive me, forgive me, forgive me."

I was so beat by the time I got to the "amen," I could hardly crawl into bed.

16

I have zero privacy.

That's what I thought the next morning when Matthew woke me up. He'd been knocking softly on my door for about ten minutes. I tried to ignore him, but he wasn't going to give up. My brother can be very persistent. I swung my legs over the side of the bed.

"What?" I said, yanking the door open.

He stuck his fingers in his mouth to point. "Look. My toof if loof."

"Matthew, that is disgusting."

"Play a game with me? I've got 'Open Sesame.' Want to watch TV? Want me to bring the TV to my room so we can watch?"

"Oh, all right," I said. "But I'll carry it up."

Dad had his feet up on the coffee table. There were holes in his socks.

"Hello," he said, not looking up from his book.

"Okay if we take the television upstairs?"

"Be my guests." Then he lifted his head suddenly. "You two going to watch TV together?"

"Sure."

"Vickie's carrying the TV upstairs," Matthew explained.

"Yeah, I see that," he said thoughtfully. "Go right ahead. Have a good time."

Matthew sat on my bed like a normal person and didn't try to hang upside down or anything bizarre like that. He is a big TV fan. He'll watch for an hour without breathing, practically. People who interrupt TV shows drive me crazy.

During a commercial for a laundry detergent *guaranteed* to get out any stain except grass and blood, Dad appeared in the doorway. "Can I see you a minute, Victoria, old girl?"

"Just wanted to say," he said, closing the door behind me, "I appreciate how you're treating Matthew. You're really growing up."

"Oh, Dad."

"No, really. Mom's told me how helpful you've been. I had to see it with my own eyes."

There is nothing worse than being complimented when you've just done something awful.

Dad's eyes sparkled in the dark hallway. "Looks

to me like your hair is growing out. Definitely getting long and lustrous."

He was kidding, of course, but I checked in the bathroom mirror just to be sure. It was a little longer.

Writing class that day also cheered me up a little. Peter was being plenty friendly, although he was plenty friendly to everyone, not just me.

We read our short stories, and his story was very good, all about a dog who saved people's lives. And it was only a Chihuahua, too. It was a lot more interesting than Cal's story about motorcycles.

Melody McClure's story was a real killer. It was set in the 1800s in England somewhere, and all these people lived in castles. The heroine's name was Violet. All the men characters were in love with her. Ted thought Melody's story was quite a tale. That's what he said, "Quite a tale."

When it was my turn, I read my story very fast because being in front of a group always makes me breathless. It was about a girl who goes ice-skating at the neighborhood rink, but no one wants her for a skating partner so she says who cares and goes to live in a cabin in the woods where she is snowed in nine months out of the year. But she doesn't mind because she is friends with all animals. It's just the girl and her cat, Weevil, and the forest animals.

I think Ted liked it. "Very imaginative," was what he called it. But sometimes it is hard to tell what he is thinking.

After class, I kind of hung around after the other kids had left.

"Anything I can help you with, Vickie?" Ted is a very helpful kind of person.

"Don't get mad, but I'd just like to know—am I an okay writer? Not great or anything, but okay at least?"

Ted didn't get mad. He put his elbows on the desk and tilted his head so he could rub the bald spot. He didn't say anything for a long time.

"Why are you asking me?" he finally said, lifting his head and twiddling his moustache.

"I figured you'd know. How do I rate, compared to other writers you know?"

"I'm quite familiar with Emily Dickinson. Compared to Emily Dickinson, you're just a beginner."

I waved him off. "I don't mean writers like Emily Dickinson. I mean writers like—like the kids in the class."

"For a girl with potential, you worry too much about how you compare with everyone else. Loosen up."

Boy, Ted must have been talking to my parents.

Disappointed, I said, "Okay, I'll try," and picked up my stuff. "See you next week."

"Hey!"

I whipped around.

"You're an okay writer," he called, putting his thumb and finger together, and holding his hand up so I could see. "A very okay writer."

17

"Baked Alaska," Dad announced, bringing dessert out to the picnic table. "Very beautiful, and *fairly* economical."

"Once again," said Mom, "a masterpiece." She smacked a mosquito on her arm.

It was a beautiful night. The sun was setting and it turned everyone's face golden. The air was warm and breathless.

"I had a session with Mrs. Champion over at Willowood today," Mom said, diving into the cake. "She cried in my arms. It almost broke my heart."

Matthew got very serious. "Why was she crying?"

"I don't know exactly. Her husband died last

year, and I suppose she's very lonely."

I knew what it was like to be lonely. That old missing-Chelsie feeling started to come back. How could I miss someone who had said such terrible things. Someone who was friends with Peggy Hiltshire.

"I've got to do more for them. Listening to their problems isn't enough. They need friends—*active* help."

Dad went inside to answer the phone.

"Where are their kids?" I asked.

"Who knows? Busy with their own lives, I suppose."

"That's not fair," I said, thinking of Mrs. Bixler.

"I could come and play a game with them," Matthew said. "Would they like to play Weasel Race?"

"They might," said Mom. "I'll see."

I sneaked a leftover hunk of bratwurst to Bullrush, who was prowling around under the table. He licked his lips and strolled away, tickling the backs of my legs with his happy, curved tail.

"I've been wondering, Mom." I was changing the subject, but it was now or never. "Don't you think it would be okay if I wore a little makeup once in a while? I mean, someone going into seventh grade—"

"*Makeup?*" Mom's voice was a squeak.

"There's this girl in my class, Betsy Bonnoff— except her pen name's Melody McClure—and she

92

wears makeup all the time. Only I wouldn't wear that much. Just a little eye shadow. And some blush. And lip gloss."

"Oh, boy. Wait till your father hears this."

Dad came back out with his hands shoved in his pockets. The screen door slammed behind him.

"The strangest thing. The restaurant says we're catering a funeral at our church, Monday. Carl said Amanda Bixler called and arranged it."

I jumped up, skinning my legs on the table.

"Don't jump to conclusions, Vickie," Mom cautioned.

I raced to the phone, my brain doing a hundred miles per hour. Punched in the numbers. One ring. Two.

Chelsie answered.

"What happened?" I yelled. "What's wrong?"

"Vic," she said in a flat voice, "my grandma's dead."

I had wished her dead.

I started praying crazily in my head, the words all melted together in a huge run-on sentence. "Dear God I didn't mean it forgive me it was a mistake she can't be dead it's my fault oh God!"

And all the while, Chelsie's voice buzzed on about a clot or a brain something or other. "She's been sick a long time," she was saying. "I guess I always expected it, but—"

I had to hang up, I said. I felt sick.

I didn't see Chelsie till the funeral. She sat up

93

front with her mom and dad, and she didn't budge a hair, hardly. I've never seen her so quiet. Mrs. Bixler kept putting her nose into a Kleenex, but she didn't blow.

I kept staring at the coffin. It was this long, shiny, coppery thing with handles. Some men wheeled it in and left it right in front of the pulpit, so you couldn't help but look at it.

"You okay?" Mom whispered, squeezing my hand.

"Sure."

Matthew squeezed my hand, too.

Some lady got up to sing. The piano was out of tune.

The pastor read some verses about green pastures. About lying down in green pastures and about the Lord always being with us. The words didn't sink in.

I felt numb and tingly. It was impossible. Grandma Warden had been alive just a few days ago. Now I was supposed to believe she was dead?

God was punishing me. He was getting me back for playing games—for wishing something I didn't really want to happen. That would teach me. I sat very, very quietly in the pew, with my sweating hands folded.

Then the pastor said, "Now we will hear a poetic tribute by Victoria Hope Mahoney, a young friend of Sapphira Warden."

I wasn't nervous. I read very loudly and very

94

slowly, and Mrs. Bixler looked up at me and started to cry. Mr. Bixler put his very large arm around her. It wasn't until I got to the end that I started to cry, too.

Afterward, I just wanted to get out of there, but my parents went right up to Mr. and Mrs. Bixler. Mom called them Herbert and Amanda and shook their hands, holding them a moment in hers. Dad just looked at his fingernails, which he does when he's nervous or embarrassed. Mrs. Bixler's eyes watered. She kind of slumped over. Mom put her arm around her shoulders, and the four of them went outside into the sunshine.

"Hi," said a voice behind me.

It was Chels. Her nose looked a little pink around the edges. She sniffed, and I dug a fresh Kleenex out of my purse.

"Stop buying these green ones," she said, blowing hard. "Green Kleenex is for nerds."

An elderly man came up to us. His eyebrows were crazy, with long hairs sprouting out of them. He got up very close and checked out our faces. It was nerve wracking.

"Chelsie and Victoria, right? Recognize you from your pictures. I'm Harold Wilkes—I was a friend of your grandma's."

I stuck my hand out. "Nice to meet you, Mr. Wilkes. Grandma liked you a lot. She told me."

"Well, she sure thought a lot of you two. And she loved your poem. She told me she wanted it read at her funeral. Beautiful, absolutely beautiful." His face got pink and he sniffed hard, dragging the back of his hand over his eyes.

I put the paper into his hands. "Keep it," I said.

Mr. Wilkes folded the poem and slid it into his jacket pocket without a word.

"Maybe," Chels said, "we could come visit you sometime. Would you mind if we came to visit you?"

He sniffed. "Do you drink coffee?"

"Do we drink coffee!" Chels said in a mock-shocked voice.

We both managed a laugh.

"Then I'd be honored. Apartment 2525. Anytime."

He went outside with his head bowed.

"Chels, I've got to talk to you."

"Me, too. Do you think your parents will let you stay over?"

"What will your mom say—?"

"Leave everything to me."

She marched outside and pulled her mother aside. Mrs. Bixler glanced at me. She even smiled a little in my direction. Then she nodded her head.

All I could think was that funerals make people act very strange. After the luncheon downstairs, Mr. and Mrs. Bixler drove me back to our house and waited in the car while I packed my stuff. Mr. Bixler got out of the driver's side and opened my door when I came out, lugging my overnight bag and sleeping bag. He put my junk in the crunk. I decided that Mr. Bixler is extremely polite.

"Your poem," said Mrs. Bixler, when I climbed into the backseat, "was lovely. I'll always remember it." She got a Kleenex and really blew her nose. It was more like a honk. Chelsie looked at me out of the corner of her eye.

I had a very good time at the Bixlers'. We watched a little TV, and Mr. Bixler showed me how to play Ping-Pong. I wasn't half bad. I beat the stuffing out of Mr. Bixler, anyway.

At bedtime, Chels and I went up to her room and opened all the windows. The crickets were going crazy.

That cool-around-the-edges Minnesota summer evening smell pushed through the screen. We leaned on the sill and didn't talk. I had felt good all afternoon, but a sadness was starting to eat at my mood. I closed my eyes. The feeling got bigger and bigger, like a headache.

"Chels?"

"Yeah? What?"

"I'm sorry for—"

"Don't say it!" she said, holding up her hand. "I thought the whole thing through, and it was my fault. It takes time to work up the nerve to admit something like that, but it's true."

"What I said was terrible. It's my fault. That's why she died."

"What are you talking about? She had a stroke. I

97

thought I told you she had a stroke."

"Yeah, but it was my fault. God is getting me back for what I said. I prayed like crazy to be forgiven, but she died anyway."

We sat cross-legged on the rug with a big bowl of M&M's between us. Neither one of us was diving in the way we normally would have.

"You didn't mean it," she pointed out, finally. "I knew that the minute you said it. Give me a break."

"That doesn't matter! You don't fool around with God."

"I think you've got God all wrong."

"Do *you* believe in God, Chelsie?"

"Well, sort of. I mean, I've been thinking about it a lot lately. Anyway, it seems to me that God doesn't work that way. Maybe it's *my* fault that Grandma died."

"*What?*"

"I covered up for Grandma. She was sick, and I didn't even tell my parents. Maybe if I had told them, Grandma would still be alive."

"You don't get sick before a stroke. A stroke just happens."

"But maybe if I had told—"

"Chels?"

"Yeah?"

"Do you mind if we pray?"

"Well, no, I guess not. What do I do?"

I told God I was very sorry. I told him I didn't blame him for wanting Grandma with him in

98

heaven. I said I was glad Chelsie and I were best bosom friends again.

"Me, too," Chelsie whispered.

I unpacked my stuff and showed Chels the new pajamas my mom had got me because, as she said, I was "becoming a young lady."

"Except Mom calls it 'a nightie.'" It was pink and covered with lace and bows. Chelsie fell over the bed laughing.

"You won't believe this," she said, and she opened her drawer and pulled out *her* new nightie. It was exactly like mine. "I *told* her I'd rather wear a big T-shirt. She thought that was terrible."

A voice from the hallway made us jump. "Time for bed, girls." For such a polite man, Chelsie's father can sound really gruff sometimes.

We snapped off the light and got into bed. The air mattress under my sleeping bag was spongy and comfortable. Chels propped herself up on an elbow. The eyelet curtain breathed in and out, and the moonlight made Chelsie's face a pale, blue shadow.

"It wasn't your fault, Old Vic," she whispered. "Grandma was ready to die. She told me."

"It wasn't your fault, either, Chels," I said softly back.

I wondered what Grandma was up to. Tonight apartment 2100, with the green walls and old couch, was empty. Grandma Warden was gone. The rooms were quiet.

I thought of my house with a little shiver of fear. Was it quiet there, too? Would Mom and Dad die? Would God leave me alone?

Dear God, I don't want to be afraid. I want to trust you, just like Grandma did. Be with me.

The verses came back. The Lord is my shepherd . . . . He makes me lie down in green pastures, he leads me beside quiet waters, he restores my soul. God loved us, Chelsie and me.

In the dark, with the pillow cool against my face and a nice summer breeze cooling me like a fan, I didn't feel afraid of death.

"Go to sleep, Old Vic. Everything's okay," said my best friend, Chelsie Bixler.

18

August will depress you if no other month does. It is the month that stores start their back-to-school advertisements. Here school is still a month away, and you have to be reminded that summer is ending and pretty soon you'll be stuck in a desk—or a gym class shower. Whoever runs the stores doesn't have to go to school.

I had August blues—bad.

That may have been the reason I promised to go with Mom to Willowood one morning. I wasn't thinking straight, plus I was a little bored. Plus, the loneliness that started the night Grandma Warden died wouldn't go away.

Mom gave me a pep talk on the way over about

being polite and not staring at the residents.

"Mom, I am not *rude,* you know."

But I did stare. I didn't mean to, but I couldn't help it. The old man she took me to visit had no teeth. He was sitting by a window, his hands in his lap. I gawked at his sunken old chin.

"Do I know you?" he asked, squinting.

That's when I would have turned and run, but Mom acted as if he were our long-lost friend.

"Actually, we're perfect strangers. I'm Bobbi Mahoney, and this is my daughter, Victoria. We just dropped by for a chat."

Right about then he grinned, his gums showing all pink and shiny. "Really? Don't just stand there. Come and sit." He fumbled around at his night-stand while we pulled up chairs. I saw him stuff something into his mouth before he turned to give us a big, toothy grin.

"Thethe thingth hurt," he lisped. He worked the dentures around with his fingers. "There. I apolo-gize for the inquisition. I always ask visitors if I know them. That's one of the hazards of old age, losing your memory. For all I knew, you might be near and dear relatives." He chortled as if it were a great joke.

I couldn't wait to get out.

There were pictures all over the bureau. Pictures of babies and little kids and weddings, and a close-up of this crazy dog with its tongue hanging out.

He gazed at Mom. "You look familiar."

"I work here—in the counseling department."

"That's it! Bobbi Mahoney. And *you!*"

I snapped to attention.

"Why does *your* name sound familiar?"

"Beats me," I said. "*I* don't work here."

Mom gave me a warning nudge.

"Victoria. Victoria." He rolled my name around on his tongue like a chocolate chip.

"I don't think we caught *your* name," my mom put in about then. "Mr.—?"

"Smith. Marvin Smith. Can you beat that for a dull name?"

"It's not the name that distinguishes a person," said Mom.

"How true, how true," said the man, smiling that awful smile again. "We lucky ones leave behind our accomplishments. Our grand deeds. Or in my case, a family."

Suddenly he heaved his body out of the chair and stumped over to the dresser. His crooked old finger pointed to a picture of a little kid. "This is Roger, number one grandson. Haven't seen him a couple of years. And this—" He held out a photograph of a girl with curly hair and a shy, sweet smile. "Oh, now, what was her name? Let's see—"

Mom and I looked at each other, cringing.

"I know! It's *Victoria!* That's why your name was so familiar." The man pointed at me happily. "Must be about your age, too. How old are you?"

"Twelve in three weeks," I answered.

"Just like my Victoria! She's about eleven and a half. And she loves cats. Kittens and cats. Do you like cats?"

"Sure. I have a cat of my own, Bullrush."

"You do?"

He came stumping back on those spindly legs, and for a minute I didn't think he was going to make it. He sat down hard in the chair.

"Listen," he said, leaning forward, "this is probably a great imposition, but I'd like to ask you a favor. Would you bring Bullrush over here for a visit? I wouldn't ask, but they don't let us keep pets, and it would mean a great deal to me. I was a great animal lover in my day."

He kind of got to me when he said that. He really did.

Mom jumped in. "What a great idea."

"What do you say, Victoria?" he asked.

"Sure. Okay."

"Wonderful!"

Mom talked awhile longer—like I said, she can be very talkative when she goes at it. Then she said it was time to go. "Anything we can do for you? get for you?"

"No, no. You've done plenty. Thank you for stopping in."

We said good-bye, and as we were heading out the door, he lifted his hand in a grand gesture and called, "Farewell, mesdemoiselles!"

19

"You wouldn't have believed it, Chels. There I was walking out the door, and what does he say? He says, 'Farewell, mesdemoiselles.' I almost died."

"Eerie."

Mr. Bixler was driving us to the mall on his way to the office. I was noticing that his neck kind of bulged out over his shirt collar. He is a very big man.

"Thank you for the ride," I said very cordially, when he pulled up in front of the main entrance.

"No problem," he said, chortling. I think Mr. Bixler has the potential of being a very jolly man.

Chels and I had some last-minute school clothes

shopping to do. I had saved up enough money to buy a pair of jeans—not the kind from Valu-Plus.

"May I help you?" asked a clerk with a name tag that said *Candy.*

"No, thank you," I said. "We're just looking." It's fun to say that when maybe you will buy something.

Candy shrugged and ambled off.

"Do you think it's a sign?" I asked. "Mr. Smith calling Mom and me mesdemoiselles?"

"I'd call it a reminder. A reminder of Grandma. I sure miss her. I think Mom does, too. Maybe the old guilt's finally getting to her."

I missed Grandma plenty.

I held up a green silk blouse with tiny pearl buttons. It was about a hundred sizes too big, definitely for someone with a chest. But no one would think you were in elementary school if you wore it.

"Are you going back to the nursing home, Vic?"

"I'm going to take Bullrush over. I promised."

"Maybe I'll go with you. It'd be good for my acting. Who knows? I might have to portray an elderly person next year in a school play."

"My youth group is starting a theater group. We practice every Thursday. Maybe you should come. We might need an old character or two, occasionally."

"That would be fun if my mom would let me. She might. She's been acting awfully weird lately."

106

Thanks to Grandma's prayers, I thought. *And mine.*

We spent an hour at the makeup counter. The clerk even let us try on some blush and junk. Chelsie overdid it. When I got done putting on a dab of periwinkle eye shadow, I looked over at her and burst out laughing.

"You look like Peggy Hiltshire!"

She squinted into the mirror on the counter. "I do, don't I? Maybe I could go with a little less." She scrubbed her cheeks with Kleenex. "How's that?"

"Very sophisticated."

I think the clerk was mad we didn't buy anything.

"After we finish shopping, Chels, want to go over to Keats? I'll show you around."

Her eyes got big. "Would you?"

"For a friend."

First thing I did was point out the room where I'd taken writing classes. It really brought back memories of old Ted. Not to mention Peter.

"These desks are great," said Chels.

Then I took her down to the cafeteria.

"Smells like pizza, heavy on the grease." She wrinkled up her nose. "Bag lunches, here I come."

We even took a gander at the gymnasium and snooped around the locker room awhile. Chels took a pantomime shower. "I'm singing in the rain," she bellowed, scrubbing her back with a make-believe brush. "Peggy says gym showers won't bother her, but if you ask me, she's bluffing."

Next we looked at ourselves in the full-length mirror plastered to the wall.

Chels scowled. "I've almost given up on getting my folks to let me wear makeup. They're hopeless." She tucked her hair behind her ear. Then she untucked it. "You know, I've been thinking about cutting my hair. What do you think? More elegant, like yours, old pal."

The hallway was dim and kind of spooky except for one office light.

Chels peeked in the door. "Ms. Runebach!"

Ms. Runebach glanced up, startled. She looked different, sitting at a big metal desk in the empty classroom, wearing jeans and those little sandals with the strap that goes between your toes. I can't stand to wear them, actually; they make my feet go crazy. But they looked great on Ms. Runebach. Her toenails were painted, I noticed. She had nice feet.

"Chelsie Bixler! Vickie Mahoney! My two favorite ex-pupils!"

Even if she was putting us on, it was a nice thing to say.

"I'm boning up," she told us with an embarrassed kind of laugh. "I took a teaching position at Keats."

"You've got to be kidding," said Chels. "That's the best news I've had all summer."

"So, I thought I'd come in and work awhile. Acclimate myself. I'm a little nervous about it."

"You, nervous?"

"Chelsie, teachers are human, too." Ms. Runebach smiled, and Chels went pink.

"Actually," I explained, covering for her, "that's why we're here, too. We were a little worried about this year, being seventh graders and all. It's been a nerve-wracking summer."

"Yes," said Ms. Runebach sympathetically. "Junior high is a big change."

"I *was* nervous," Chels jumped in, "but I got over it. I'm looking forward to seventh grade, if you want to know the truth."

The rat.

"Well, it you ever need any help, I hope you'll feel free to stop in."

"Thanks, Ms. Runebach," I said.

"We will," said Chelsie.

"That was a smart crack," I said when we got outside. " *I'm looking forward to seventh grade, Ms. Runebach!* Since when?"

"She's such a classy lady, I didn't want her to think I was afraid. She would never have understood."

"She was in seventh grade once, you know. Everyone was in seventh grade once."

"Ms. Runebach, a squirrelly seventh grader?"

I thought about it. "She was probably a very unsquirrelly seventh grader."

"You know what? I'm dying for a malt. Absolutely dying."

Never one to turn down a malt, I headed with

her toward Otto's. It's a place in our neighborhood that could use a good coat of paint, but it couldn't make better butter brickle malts if it were in The Circle.

"I'll buy yours," I said generously.

"No need." Chels dug around in her pocket and pulled out a couple dollars. "I'm loaded. Well, sort of loaded."

"Where'd you get that?"

"Mom got this idea suddenly that I needed to learn a little responsibility. So I've been baby-sitting the last couple weeks. Come on, let me get you a malt. Kind of a peace offering."

I started to argue, something I have noticed adults do when someone tries to buy things for them. But then I decided no, it would make old Chels feel better to buy something for me.

Otto's malts are huge, but we each ordered one and sat in the shade to drink them. We practically had to shout to hear over the blasting music.

"Isn't it great about Ms. Runebach?" said Chels.

"Maybe we'll have English class with her some-day. Just like old times. Hey, did you get your class schedule yet? Maybe we have a class together."

"I've been carrying it around for a week." She pulled out a crumpled paper, and I leaned over her shoulder while she compared them.

"No. Yeah. Wait. Humanities. First hour."

I could hardly believe it.

"Now, the only thing we haven't solved," I

reminded her, "is the gym shower thing."

"Vic, I have come to the conclusion that some things you just have to let happen. 'When you walk through a storm, hold your head up high.' That's from *Carousel*. Anyway, some things you just have to face head-on."

"The other thing I have heard is that it is definitely not chic to be a Christian in junior high. I'm going to have to stand up for what I believe."

"Like this?" Chels jumped up on a bench. "Fourscore and seven—" she yelled.

"Get down! Everyone's staring at you."

"Let 'em. I'm not embarrassed. I'm pretty good looking, actually. If you don't count braces." She balanced on her toes like a trapeze artist. "But, Vic. You're not going to turn into an evangelist on me, are you? Just what I need. A friend who preaches in the halls."

"I'm not like that!" I said angrily. "I just want to be myself."

"We're not talking about little Lonsdale Elementary here. This is junior high."

"I *know*."

"It won't be as easy as you think."

I took a deep breath. "I know."

"Vic," said Chels, putting her hand on my shoulder. "I want you to know I really think you've got guts."

"Potential," I said. "I have great potential."

20

We all chipped in and got Ted a T-shirt that said, "Kiss Me. I Read Emily Dickinson." I think he would die if anyone really did kiss him. He said he loved the T-shirt, anyway.

"Our last class together," he said, making a tragic face. "I hope you can all say you've learned something."

Cal waved his hand. "I've learned how to write a mean haiku."

"The only poet to ever write an ode to a Harley-Davidson in traditional Japanese verse form," said Ted, rolling his eyes.

"Will you be back at Keats this fall?" Peter wanted to know.

"Afraid not. I'm getting married in September—to a wonderful woman named Sylvia. We're moving to New York City."

"How romantic," said Melody.

"I've always wanted to go to New York," I said. "Maybe I could come for a visit sometime."

"By all means," he said, sounding as though he really meant it. "We'll show you the sights."

"It might take me awhile to save up."

"Well, if nothing else, I'll see your name in all the New York bookstores."

I grinned. "Right," I said.

21

The roller-skating was Chelsie's idea. She was even going to invite Peggy Hiltshire.

"What for? She's such a phony."

"Give her a chance. You don't know her very well, and I think she's lonely."

I felt guilty. "Okay. Ask her."

"Dad's driving. See you at seven."

I spent about three hours putting on the eye shadow Mom had picked up for me. It looked pretty good, actually.

"What's on your eyelids?" Matthew stood on tiptoe to see better in the bad bathroom light.

"Makeup."

"It looks good."

I gave him the once-over to see if it was a wise-crack, but he just looked at me, blinking. I kind of squeezed his elbow. It wasn't really a pinch.

"Matthew, old boy, you're getting to be pretty decent."

I went downstairs in my new jeans and the eye shadow. Dad looked at me quickly and went back to stirring his Bernaise sauce. One thing about my dad. He can be very sensitive.

"Taste," he said, holding out a wooden spoon, his hand cupped underneath. "Where are you off to?"

"Roller-skating. Don't ask me why. I promised Chelsie."

"You'll be the belle," he said. "Man, I remember my roller-skating days."

"Do you?" Mom seemed very interested.

"Bless your jealous little heart."

They kissed.

The phone rang, and Mom went to answer it.

I took one last look in the bathroom mirror. When I smiled, my teeth looked very white, and my face looked very happy. I did it again, just for the effect.

"Well, if that doesn't beat all," said my mother, fresh off the phone. "That was Amanda Bixler. She wants to volunteer at Willowood. I suggested she help teach the craft classes. I think she'd be good with that."

"What brought this on?" Dad asked.

"Maybe she's lonely," Mom said, standing in the

115

doorway and braiding a couple strands of hair. "Maybe she misses her mother. There was something wrong between them; I'm not sure what. Maybe she's coming around. I'll bet she gets real lonely with Herbert always at work. It just goes to show that everyone needs to do something worthwhile. And that people eventually come around. They almost always do."

Dear God, I prayed. *Thanks*.

At 7:00, Chels showed up at the door.

"Are you ready? You look great. Don't be nervous, Vic—this will be good for you."

"Hi, Peggy," I said, climbing into the backseat. "What's that perfume you're wearing?"

"Do you like it? It's just a little ol' something Chels and I picked up earlier this summer. The day we tried on every perfume in the store."

Little ol'. I rolled my eyes, but not so Peggy saw. "I could use some cologne myself," I said pleasantly.

"Want to check out the perfume counter? We could all go tomorrow, if you don't have anything planned."

"I'm available," said Chelsie from the front seat. "What about you, Vic?"

"Me, too," I said.

The rink was packed. I checked my pocket to make sure the five was still there—in case I needed to make an emergency escape to the snack bar.

"You can go faster than that!" Chels yelled, whipping past me on her skates. I chased her at full

116

speed for a couple of laps. Even Peggy joined in.

I was just starting to have a good time when the announcer bawled, "Time for an old-fashioned Snowball Skate! Girls on the left, boys on the right."

"Come back here!" Chels called after me, as I whizzed past the line of girls starting to form.

The only good thing about the Snowball is that there are no lines at the snack bar. But the hot dog was rubbery, and I chewed slowly, watching couple after graceful couple skate around in the dark. The disco ball flashed all over them.

Suddenly I felt I was being watched. I whipped around, and sure enough, there was this shape staring at me in the dark.

"Hi," said the shape, moving closer.

"Oh, *Peter*. Now I recognize you."

"The glasses, right?" he asked, laughing. "They're a real tip-off."

I heard myself laugh this stupid laugh. I'd have to watch that.

"What are you doing here?" he asked.

"My friend, Chelsie Bixler, wanted me to come. I'm not a big roller-skating fan, if you want to know the truth."

"I'm kind of *into* roller-skating, myself."

Peter sat down at the snack bar with me, and my hands got so jittery I could hardly hold onto the hot dog bun. I wondered if my eye shadow was on straight, although it was so dark in there he probably couldn't see it anyway.

117

"So," he said, "you going to Pauline's party?"

"Sure. Are you?"

"Yeah. Maybe I'll see you there."

"Yeah."

"I wish school would never start. You know what I mean?"

I knew. "It was a great summer."

"Especially Ted's class."

"Do you want to be a writer?"

"I don't know," he answered. "I like sports. I'm heavily into soccer and softball."

The Snowball was over, and the lights were coming back on. Peter wasn't looking at me anymore.

I wrapped up the hot dog in the wrapper and was quiet for a minute. Then I said, "You know how I said I don't like skating? I do like it once in a while, you know?"

He looked the other way. "What about now?"

My hands stopped sweating after the first song. He could really skate. On corners he crossed one foot over the other. Peggy and Chelsie had their mouths open as I whipped around the crowded rink, holding hands with Peter, the poet.

"Debonair," Chels said, on the way home, a code word that of course Mr. Bixler and Peggy didn't understand. "Yes, indeed. Junior high is starting to look better all the time."

22

A few days later, I got the note.

I had gone outside to get the mail for Mom. As usual I tossed the envelopes on the counter without even looking at them. I never get mail, probably due to the fact that I never write any letters. Anyway, Mom called after me, "Hey, don't you want your mail?"

It was a little yellow envelope that said "Ms. Victoria Mahoney" on it.

Inside there was a note from my old teacher, written in her tiny handwriting.

"Dear Vickie, Good luck in the seventh grade. You have great talent; don't ever forget that. And don't forget all the grammar I taught you.

Sincerely, Grace Runebach." Grace. I couldn't believe it.

"That's my girl," Dad said when he read it. "This Ms. Runebach is a very discerning individual."

"She's got you pegged," Mom seconded.

Chelsie got a note, too. It said that she was an actress of real distinction. Ms. Runebach said she would be looking for her in all of Keats's drama productions, which made Chels feel like one million bucks.

"Do you suppose she's right?" she asked me, from her private phone. "Do you suppose we really will have a great time in seventh grade? Ms. Runebach has never been wrong before."

"Whatever happens, Chels," I told her, "we can handle it."

And I almost believed it myself.